I059E765

THE BOTTOM
OF THE 9th

Copyright © 2014 Anthony Giangregorio

ISBN Softcover ISBN 13: 978-1-61199-092-8
                ISBN 10: 1-611990-92-0
All stories contained in this book have been published with permission
from the authors.

All rights reserved. No part of this book may be reproduced or transmit-
ted in any form or by any means, electronic or mechanical, including
photocopying, recording, or by any information storage and retrieval
system, without permission in writing from the copyright owner.

This is a work of fiction.

Names, characters, places and incidents either are the product of the
author's imagination or are used fictitiously, and any resemblance to any
actual persons, living or dead, events, or locales is entirely coincidental.

This book was printed in the United States of America.

For more info on obtaining additional copies of this book, contact:
www.livingdeadpress.com

THE BOTTOM OF THE 9th

ANTHONY GIANGREGORIO

MORE LIVING DEAD PRESS BOOKS

THE TURNING: A STORY OF THE LIVING DEAD * MEN OF PERDITION
THE DEAD OF SPACE BOOK 1 & 2 * THE BABYLONIAN CURSE
PLAYING GOD: A ZOMBIE NOVEL * THE JUNKYARD
SUPERHEROES VS. ZOMBIES
PLANET OF THE DEAD: Vol 1-3 * THE HAUNTED THEATRE
ZOMBIES IN OUR HOMETOWN * ATOMIC ZOMBIES
UNITED STATES OF ARMAGEDDON
THE Z WORD * REVIEWS OF THE DEAD
NIGHT OF THE WOLF: A WEREWOLF ANTHOLOGY
JUST BEFORE NIGHT: A ZOMBIE ANTHOLOGY
THE BOOK OF HORROR 1 & 2
THE WAR AGAINST THEM: A ZOMBIE NOVEL
CHILDREN OF THE VOID * DARK DREAMS
BLOOD RAGE & DEAD RAGE (BOOK 1& 2 OF THE RAGE VIRUS SERIES)
DEAD MOURNING: A ZOMBIE HORROR STORY
BOOK OF THE DEAD: A ZOMBIE ANTHOLOGY VOLUME 1-6
LOVE IS DEAD: A ZOMBIE ANTHOLOGY
ETERNAL NIGHT: A VAMPIRE ANTHOLOGY
END OF DAYS: AN APOCALYPTIC ANTHOLOGY VOLUME 1-5
THE ZOMBIE IN THE BASEMENT (FOR ALL AGES)
DEAD WORLDS: UNDEAD STORIES VOLUMES 1-7
FAMILY OF THE DEAD * REVOLUTION OF THE DEAD
KINGDOM OF THE DEAD * DEAD HISTORY: Vol 1 &2
THE MONSTER UNDER THE BED * DEAD THINGS
DEAD TALES: SHORT STORIES TO DIE FOR
ROAD KILL: A ZOMBIE TALE * DEADFREEZE * DEADFALL
SOUL EATER * THE DARK * RISE OF THE DEAD
DEAD END: A ZOMBIE NOVEL * VISIONS OF THE DEAD
BOOK OF CANNIBALS VOLUME 2 * CHRISTMAS IS DEAD…AGAIN
EMAILS OF THE DEAD * CHILDREN OF THE DEAD
TALES OF THE DEAD * TALES OF BIGFOOT
NOVELLAS OF THE DEAD * TEN SILLY ZOMBIES JUMPING ON THE BED
ZOMBIES ARE COOL * ZOMBIES ARE PEOPLE TOO

THE DEADWATER SERIES

DEADWATER * DEADWATER: Expanded Edition
DEADRAIN * DEADCITY * DEADWAVE * DEAD HARVEST
DEAD UNION * DEAD VALLEY * DEAD TOWN/ HOMEWARD BOUND
DEAD GRAVE * DEAD SALVATION * DEAD ARMY

Table of Contents

FOREWORD

INSPIRATION WHERE YOU LEAST EXPECT IT

So I'm at the Pop Culture convention in Wilmington, MA a few months ago. My table is set up with all my books, shelving as well, and once done, I get to sit down and take a breather.

Well, the first thing I do after setting up, is to see who's around me, such as artists, or toy vendors.

See, I love the conventions for the opportunities it provides me, such as potential for networking. I did a horror show last year and met an artist who does incredible drawings of zombie women. They're so perfect anyone who didn't realize it, would assume the drawings were really women with makeup on, then photo-graphed.

Well, we talked and I ended up making a calendar with him for 2014 through Living Dead Press, which was a great success, I might add.

At that same show I met a guy who dresses up as an evil clown and does parties and the like. At first when he passed my table while doing his rounds of the convention, all I did was shudder inwardly. I mean, who wouldn't be freaked out by a clown, and an evil one at that?

Each time he would pass my table over the weekend, we would talk a little, saying this and that as he strolled by. Then finally, near the end of the weekend, and he was passing me once more, and I told him he was freaking me the hell out, I was suddenly inspired to do an anthology about evil clowns.

After talking with him, I got permission to use his likeness on the cover. I then reached out to some like-minded authors who thought it would be fun, and now I have an evil clown anthology made though LDP as well. See, for me, inspiration comes from everywhere, and I'm always looking for it to strike.

So, back to the Pop Culture convention mentioned above. I get sidetracked easily, as you can imagine.

I was alone manning my table on the first day of the convention, so not wanting to leave my table unattended, the other vendors either beside me or right across from me are usually the people I will hover around, as that way my table is still in clear view — in case a passing customer stops by my table to check out the books on display.

Well, across from me was a guy with a rather simple looking table. He had a laptop playing something I had no idea what it was, and a few books scattered on the table. Seeing a fellow writer, I wandered over to chat and I found out that this man, who went by the name Kevin Baldwin, writes plays in his spare time. As we began to chat, the laptop was pointed out, and that was when I was informed that some of his plays had actually been made with actors and everything.

Is he on Broadway? No, not yet, but the future is an open-ended creature, is it not? So anyway, we're talking about this and that, and though I'm interested, plays aren't my thing, but I still found it impressive that he got something he wrote made into a living play.

And that was when he pointed out one play in particular, one about an old man who goes to a ball game and interacts with the fans, only for the reader to find out that the fans are actually his memories and that the man is suffering from Alzheimer's disease. Now, before I go further, I need to point something out. I personally have been fortunate enough in my life to never have had to deal with a family member or friend who was dealing with Alzheimer's, so the fact that when he pointed the play out to me and I felt like I'd been hit with a ton of bricks is an understatement.

But for some unknown reason, his play really resonated with me on an emotional level. I guess it's the idea of being someone suffering from the disease and then slowly losing themselves in it. After all, without their memories, is a person really a person?

What makes us who we are, our soul, is in many ways comprised of who we are and the memories we have made over the years of our life. The memories are what form us into the individuals we become. So to lose that, and have absolutely no control over it, well, it scares me way more than a horde of zombies ever could. To me, Alzheimer's disease is worse than death.

At least when you die it's over, lights out, good night. But to have this disease, to slowly begin losing yourself, and no matter how hard you want to fight, there's no way you can prevent it, and that in the end, whoever you are will simply fade away, leaving behind the shell that was you, well, that's more terrifying than any horror book I've ever read or written.

So, I've explained that this disease terrifies me the way nothing else—even death itself—does. The play Kevin created blew me away, to the point that if I'd been some well-respected director, his play would now be getting optioned for a movie.

But I'm not a great director; I'm just a writer, so I did the next best thing. I got together with Kevin, and with his play for inspiration, I put it into book form.

Whether or not the story hits you as emotionally it did me is irrelevant. This play needed to be made into a book, so that others can enjoy it and appreciate the genius of what Kevin created, and now with my help, I hope I've made that happen.

For some reason I can't really explain, this story of a man losing himself from within emotionally inspired me the way few things have in my lifetime.

I hope you enjoy the story as much as I did upon first discovering it, and the next time you recall a memory of years' past as it flutters through your mind, don't just brush it away.

Cherish it, because like so many things in life, it may not be there the next time you look.

Anthony Giangregorio
July 2104

THE BOTTOM OF THE 9th

The sun was high, a few sparse clouds marring the otherwise pristine blue sky. It was summer; not just by the temperature of the weather but by the way people acted towards one another. There was something special about a summer day that was unlike anything else in New England. After suffering inside homes for the winter—which seemed to take longer to end each year—New Englanders all across the joining states knew that the days of summer were finite, and before they knew it, the cold arms of winter would be back again.

But not for months.

Today it was beautiful out: around seventy-five degrees with a light wind, the humidity low and comfortable. Tomorrow it might be ninety with one hundred percent humidity, with the air so hot that to stand in the shade would cause a person to sweat.

Not today though.

Today it was a great day to be alive, and an ever better day for a baseball game.

The bleachers behind first base were half-filled, an amalgam of faces and races sitting side by side, everyone laughing and smiling. Massachusetts was a melting pot of all nations, from Spanish to African American to Latino, to Irish and Italian, and Millborough, MA was no different.

Everyone was enjoying a relaxing time watching the children's baseball game.

Some spectators held up signs, such as: **"GO, TEAM, GO!"** and **"Millborough #1"**

Most of the spectators were calling and yelling at their team, while others were sitting quietly, content to let the more rambunctious do the lion's share of the cheering.

The bleachers themselves were covered in graffiti, and here and there the wooden planks people walked and sat on were in disrepair. The bleachers looked old, worn, as if they had been exposed to countless years of weather.

If any of the fans minded, none showed it, all concentrating on the game and their team.

In a section directly across from first base were a collection of such fans.

On the first row, so he could get the best possible view, was a man wearing a baseball cap. Behind him, in the third row, was a woman wearing blue jeans. A man wearing tan slacks was situated in the third row to the left side of the middle section, and at the top of the bleachers, so they could get what they felt was a better view than Baseball Cap, sat two women, one wearing a red sweater vest, despite the nice day, and the second a pink jogging suit. On the cracked and peeling plank at their feet, between them, was a cooler full of sandwiches and drinks.

All eyes were focused on the game as the next batter walked up to the plate. A few catcalls could be heard from other parts of the crowd, but this little section had only positive people, who were just happy to be at the game. Did they want their team to win? Of course they did, but before that came the simple joy of being at a game, with either friends or like-minded people around them.

Unobserved for the moment, as everyone watched the game, no one noticed an old man enter the bleachers from the right. He looked disheveled, his gray hair uncombed, his sagging jaw needing a shave. He had been handsome once, but now he looked rather beaten down, as if the same weather and time that had worn away the paint from the bleachers had done the same thing to him.

He seemed lost, as if he didn't know where he was, and had only stumbled onto the ballgame by accident. His age was anywhere from late fifties to late sixties, but in truth, he could have been older or younger; his face was difficult to discern without more information of who he was.

He wore a simple pair of brown pants and a gray sweatshirt, both looking as if the man had slept in them the previous night.

What was odd was that he wore no shoes on his feet, and they were dirty from his trek through the dirt that separated the parking lot from the bleachers.

The sound of a bat striking a baseball filled the air, and all the fans jumped up as one as the old man stared in confusion, looking even more disoriented.

"Yeah! That's it! Run it! Run it! Run it!" Baseball Cap yelled, his face alight with joy as he pumped his right hand in the air. All around him the other fans were cheering as well, each yelling positive things at the runner.

"Go! Go! Go! You got it!" Blue Jeans called, clapping and bouncing in her seat. Her eyes were wide with excitement, her gaze locked on the runner as the player made his way to first base.

Slacks quickly added his voice to the mix with, "Throw it to second! Double play! Come on! Throw it to second!" He paused for a heartbeat and then added, "Okay, then, throw it to third! Throw it to third!" Evidently, Slacks was rooting for the opposing team, not that any of the others minded. It was all good fun and Slacks was as welcome as anyone else.

"Okay, he's safe. They're all safe," Blue jeans said, most of the spectators clapping in support of the team. "All right, guys. Good play. Good play." She sat back down, shifting her butt slightly to get better situated. Her face was red from the excitement and she had a healthy glow on her features. Like the other fans, she was perspiring in the hot sun.

"They're all safe. One, two and three. Good hit! Good hit!" Sweater vest said, clapping louder than some of the people around her. Her complexion was slightly red, too, as if she'd been out in the sun for too long, which she probably had.

The old man stopped climbing the bleachers and stood in the center of the spectators, his gaze going out to the field. He rubbed his chin in confusion, his eyes then turning away from the field to take in the people around him. "What is this? What's going on?" he asked, his voice hoarse, his breath coming in slight gasps as he recovered from the climb up the bleachers. His mouth was open as he began to breathe faster.

"Hey, Pops! It's about time you showed up," Blue jeans said, waving to the old man.

"There you are! Where have you been?" Baseball Cap added. "Here; sit beside me. I saved you a spot." He patted the place on the bleachers next to him, but Pops didn't move, he only continued to stare out onto the field.

"We've been waiting for you," Blue Jeans added.

"You missed nearly half the game," Slacks chimed in. He glanced down at his pants and made sure his slacks were still neat, the crease in the front of each leg tight, and that there were no stains evident.

"Game? What game?" Pops said, sitting down where he was to rest his tired body. He was exhausted, but he didn't remember why. "Do I know you people? I don't think I do, none of you look familiar."

"Man, it sure is wicked hot out today," Jogging suit said, as she wiped her arm across her perspiring brow. She called out to the old man, "Did you bring any munchies there, ya old geezer?" She laughed as she said it, though no one else thought it was funny. When she realized no one else liked her joke, she frowned deeply, almost pouting.

Sweater vest nudged Jogging suit to get the woman's attention, then pointed to the cooler at their feet. "Never mind that, silly. I have some sandwiches right here. Don't you remember I made sure to bring them when you picked me up to take me to the game?"

Jogging suit looked around while scratching her head. "I did? I don't remember that. Are you sure? If so, then where's the grub?"

"In the cooler. Here," Sweater vest said. "It's right here for Heaven's sake."

"Good. Because I'm hungry as hell. I could eat a horse I'm so hungry," she replied.

"Big surprise there," her partner rebutted, a smirk on her lips. Jogging Suit turned to look at her friend but said nothing, choosing to ignore the remark and be the better person.

There was the sound of the cracking of a bat and once more all conversation stopped and everyone stood up, clapping and calling out, a few booing from another part of the bleachers.

"Hey, you guys knock that off! We're all here to have fun!" Jogging suit yelled.

"Yeah," Sweater vest added in support of her friend, "We don't need that kind of attitude here."

"Foul ball! Foul ball!" the umpire yelled as he walked around home plate. He pulled out a small brush and wiped the plate clean of dust, then stepped back to give the batter room.

In the bleachers, most of the fans sat down, almost all of them looking disappointed, more than a few grumbling to each other.

"Figures," Slacks said. "Just two and a half feet more and it would've been a good hit."

"That's okay!" Blue Jeans shouted. "That's okay, son. You'll get 'em next time, batter!"

"What is this? Who's playing?" Pops asked as he stared at the field. He didn't recognize any of the teams. There's a game playing today? Since when?

"Strike three, you're out!" the umpire yelled and the batter walked off the field, more than a few boos and cheers following the player.

Blue Jeans pointed to home plate as the next player walked up to bat. "The next kid is up," she said, ignoring Pops' question.

"Bring 'em home, batter!" Baseball Cap shouted. "You got this!"

"Is anyone listening to me?" Pops' eyes squinted in thought as he tried to recall what he'd been doing before coming to the game. "I was heading east on Winchester Street, running an errand. I was going to the store for some bread and milk. But if I was doing that, then how did I get here?"

"Easy out, pitcher! Easy out!" Jogging suit yelled as the next batter came up to the plate. "This guy's a pushover!"

"Or was I going west on Elm?" Pops said, shaking his head as if he was trying to clear it. "Damn it, I don't remember what I was doing. Why can't I remember?"

"Shut up already and let the kid bat!" Sweater vest said to Jogging suit, punching the woman in the arm.

Jogging suit laughed at her friend at being playfully hit and replied, "Take it easy! I was just jokin' around. I like that kid, he's good for the team."

Pops looked around at the faces of the people around him, his gaze resting on each one for a moment before moving on. "Do I know any of you? I don't think I do, but my memory's kind of fuzzy for some reason." Once more he was ignored by the fans; they were all focused on the ballgame.

"Three more runs and we can all go home," Slacks said as he clapped. "Three more to go!"

"Come on, batter! Get a hit!" Jogging suit yelled, whistling loudly with her fingers in her mouth. Sweater vest winced, the sound too close to her head. She glared at Jogging suit but said nothing. The two women had been friends for years and Sweater vest knew how annoying Jogging suit could be.

Pops stared out at the field, not really seeing it, still lost in thought. There was the hint of a memory fluttering at the back of his mind, but like candle smoke in the wind, it was there one moment and gone the next. He tried to focus his mind on the image peering out from the shadows of his mind but it just wouldn't come forth. He wanted to cry out but held his tongue.

"Third base is leading!" Jogging suit shouted. "Watch it, kid!" She pointed to the player at home plate about to begin batting. "Outfield has got you pegged if you don't pay attention."

The pitcher let fly, and a second later the crack of bat meeting a baseball filled the air. The spectators jumped to their feet, hooting and hollering.

But no sooner did the excitement build than the umpire cried out, "Foul ball!"

Like a slate had been wiped clean, most of the fans visages went from elation to disappointment. Many looked like they'd just lost their family dog.

"Man, I really thought he got a piece of that one," Jogging Suit said, dejected.

"It was close," Sweater vest replied. "A few more to the left and it would've been good."

Blue jeans clapped from a few seats below the two women. She was attending the game alone, but was still having a good time. She knew everyone was friendly from past games and it wouldn't take much to get everyone in a section to start chatting with one another—especially if the topic was about the game and the players.

"I don't see anything out there. Did you say there's a game playing?" Pops asked as he looked out onto the field. He squinted some more, as if that would help. "Where are the players?"

"Cataracts, huh, Pops? Geez, that must suck," Sweater vest said upon hearing Pops. "My grandma has those and she can't see the newspaper when it's three inches in front of her face. I've got to read to her all the time now."

"He doesn't have cataracts," Baseball Cap said as he studied the old man. He pointed to Pops' feet. "He also doesn't have anything on his feet."

"What're you talking about?" Pops asked.

"What did you do, Pops?" Baseball Cap asked jokingly. "Did you forget... those... those..." He hesitated, trying to recall the name for footwear. "Those things that go on your feet?" He began to cough, hard, and he shook his head and touched his forehead with the palm of his hand. "Sheesh, I must be coming down with something. I suddenly don't feel so good."

"You okay, buddy?" Jogging suit asked, interested.

"Huh? Oh yeah. Sure. I'm fine now. That was weird, though," Baseball cap said. "It was like a wave of nausea hit me."

"What things are you talking about?" Pops asked, staring at Baseball cap.

Snapping his fingers as he looked up at the sky, Baseball Cap tried to recall the word he was looking for. "Those...things. The things you put on your feet." Then he remembered and his eyes lit up with recognition. "Shoes. That's it. Shoes!"

Pops glanced down at his bare feet, as if for the first time. He wiggled his toes, as if the digits were saying high to him. "I'm not sure exactly." He paused in thought. "Shoes?" He looked over at Baseball cap and asked, "Have we met before?"

The crack of the bat was heard again, and almost every fan in the bleachers jumped to their feet, clapping and hollering in excitement, cheering the runner on.

"He got a piece of that one!" Baseball Cap yelled, forgetting about Pops, his eyes only on the game. "Nice hit, too!"

"All right! Go! You got this!" Blue jeans called out loudly.

"Throw it home! Throw it home!" Jogging suit screamed. "Catcher! Run for it!"

"Hey! Maybe we should go sit on the bleachers at the other side of the field!" Sweater vest suggested to Jogging suit "We'd get a better view over there."

"Uh-uh, I don't want to," Jogging suit replied.

"Why not?"

Jogging suit shrugged. "The food's better on this side. Especially the hot dogs."

Sweater vest laughed and punched her friend playfully on the arm again.

"Ow, will you cut it out?" Jogging suit snapped.

"Safe!" the umpire yelled.

"He's safe," Blue jeans said to anyone who would listen. "You hear that? He's safe." She leaned forward and yelled out to the player who was safe. "You're safe, Joey! Good job! Way to hustle it!"

"Two runs scored. It's nine to nine," Slacks volunteered.

17

"Yup. Runners are safe at first and third," Baseball Cap added.

Pops frowned as he considered his surroundings. "I think I hate baseball," he stated flatly.

"Good play! Good play!" Baseball Cap called, clapping as well.

Pops turned to face Baseball cap, and when the younger man turned to Pops, as if sensing someone was watching him, Pops asked, "Are you my son?"

"You kids are awesome! Good going, Joey! Good going!" Blue Jeans called, whistling long and loud so she could be heard over the rest of the spectators.

"How many outs?" Sweater vest asked, her question for anyone who was listening.

"Only one," Jogging suit replied.

"What inning is this?" Pops asked.

"Huh?" Baseball Cap said. As the closest person to Pops, he was able to hear the old man's question.

"I said; what inning is it?"

Baseball Cap waited a second before replying, "Oh, I..." He paused and coughed again. "You know what? I'm not exactly sure."

"It's the bottom of the sixth," Blue jeans said. She wanted to make a friend, as she was having a good time and now wished she hadn't come to the game alone.

Slacks began searching for his notebook, where he kept all relevant information on the players and games. "The next kid has an RBI of seventeen," he said after finding and reading the page he wanted.

"You keeping track?" Blue Jeans asked. "Geez, they're seven years old, for Christ's sake."

Slacks gave her a shrug. "It's never too early to keep good records."

"These boys lose track of how many times they go to the fridge to get something to eat or miss the toilet. You really think they can keep track of their batting averages?" Blue jeans prodded.

"That reminds me. I'm hungry," Jogging suit said loudly, as if everyone around her should know this, too.

Sweater vest sighed. "Really? *That* reminded you you're hungry?"

Jogging suit frowned. "Just shut up and give me a sandwich."

"You're always eating," was her friend's reply.

"And you're always a pain. Give me a damn sandwich. Wow, it's hot out here!" Jogging suit complained as she wiped her brow with the back of her sleeve.

"You know, I can't remember if I ate this morning," Pops said. "That's weird."

Jogging suit grabbed two sandwiches out of the cooler, and keeping one for herself, she walked down the bleachers to where Pops was. "Hey, mister! Hey, mister! Ya want a sandwich? We have plenty over here." She handed one of the sandwiches to the old man while eating the second one.

Sweater vest gave her friend such a scowl it could have peeled paint off a car. "Cut it out. Don't go giving away all our food."

"Ah, shut up, you. I'm just being nice," she told her friend and then turned back to Pops. "Go ahead, mister. My treat."

Pops took the sandwich. "Thank you. That's very nice of you."

"Hey, no problem. My momma raised her little girl right."

"She acts like she was the one who made them or something," Sweater vest said. "I'm the one who made them this morning."

Pops began eating the sandwich, stuffing his mouth with each bite.

"Hey now, you want a punch in the nose," Jogging suit quipped. "I could've made those sandwiches but you volunteered."

"Fat chance," came her friend's reply. "You'd burn a salad if you tried to make one. You're terrible in the kitchen." Sweater vest smirked proudly upon getting the upper hand, then she let out a bark of laughter.

"You want a napkin, Pops?" Baseball Cap asked.

Pops shook his head no; he was fine, despite the fact mayonnaise was all over his upper lip and chin.

"What do you mean by laughing?" Jogging suit asked, not willing to let the subject go so easily.

"You heard me. You can't even remember your own name and you think you're gonna go and cook?"

"I can so remember it."

"Oh yeah? Let's see you."

"Fine," Jogging suit said.

"Fine," Sweater vest repeated.

Jogging suit began to think, her forehead creasing in concentration. After a long pause she finally said, "Yeah, I got nothing."

"See! I told you so," Sweater vest said cheerily.

"Okay. What's yours then, smartass?"

Sweater vest stopped laughing and began to think herself. Her lips turned into a frown as she began to think carefully. After quite a long pause she replied, "Ummm... Cinderella."

Some of the nearby spectators laughed at that, assuming it was all a joke.

Jogging suit took a bite out of her sandwich, chewed a few times and called out to Pops. "Hey, mister. How old are you anyway?"

Pops had finished his sandwich and was wiping his mouth on his sleeve. At the question, he turned to face the woman and said without hesitation, "I'm forty-seven."

Some of the surrounding fans laughed at that and Pops frowned, as if they knew something he didn't. "On second thought, I think I'm fifty-seven. Right?"

"Don't believe him," Baseball Cap said to anyone who was listening. "He's sixty-three."

"No, he's sixty-six," Slacks said, jumping into the conversation.

"He is?" Baseball Cap asked.

"I am?" Pops asked as well.

21

"Yes." Slacks told Baseball cap "He is." He swiveled in his seat to face Pops and reiterated, "You are, Pops."

"Don't worry, mister," Blue jeans consoled. "You look great for your age, no matter what anyone says."

"Hey, you want another sandwich there, old timer?" Jogging suit asked.

"No thank you," Pops said. "There, uh, certainly was a lot of mayonnaise in mine."

Jogging suit turned in her seat to look Sweater vest square in the eye. "See? I told you there was too much mayo in those sandwiches."

Sweater vest shrugged "Your arms ain't broken. You could have made the sandwiches instead of me," she said sarcastically.

Jogging suit waved a hand before her, as if the subject was moot. "Nah…I can't. I forgot the recipe."

Sweater vest did a double take. "Recipe? It's a sandwich."

Jogging suit glanced down at her feet, a look of insecurity crossing her features. "Anyway, you make 'em better than I can. Always did."

"Aww, thanks. That's nice of you to say."

Pops leaned closer to Baseball cap to get the man's attention. "I did eat, didn't I?"

"Wow. Talk about forgetful," Slacks commented at overhearing Pops.

Pops turned to look at Slacks and said, "Well, I…"

"No, not you, old man," Slacks said, cutting Pops off. "I meant the umpire. He forgot to clean the plate at home. What an idiot."

"Hey, pal, why don't you write to Better Homes and Gardens about it?" Jogging suit quipped at Slacks.

"Now, now. We're all on the same side," Blue jeans said.

The umpire stood on home plate to address the crowd. "Now coming to the plate: number 51!"

"Just great," Jogging suit said but then looked out at the field. "Here comes that fat Walker kid up to bat."

"That's not a very nice thing to say. What do you..." Blue jeans began, but was cut off midsentence.

"Just wait for it," Jogging suit said as the pitcher threw a fastball to Walker.

"Strike one!" the umpire yelled.

"Oh, my," Blue jeans said as the batter swung and missed.

"See what I mean?" Jogging suit said with a knowing smile.

Sweater vest leaned forward in her seat and called out to Slacks, "Hey you! Record keeper. Has that kid ever gotten a hit?"

Slacks checked his notebook. "Let's see. In three years of play..." He found the page he wanted and used his index finger to find Walker's stats. Armed with the knowledge, he closed the notebook and put it away. "Nope. The only part of the ball he ever got was the breeze."

"Strike two!" the umpire yelled, his strong voice cutting through the chatter of the fans.

"Oh, dear," Blue jeans said. "That's too bad."

"Then why..." Sweater vest began but was cut off.

"Wait for it," Slacks and Jogging suit said simultaneously.

"Strike three!" the umpire yelled. "You're outta there!"

Jogging suit sighed. "Man, I really hate the *mandatory play rule*."

Without warning, the sunlight suddenly disappeared, bathing the field in darkness. It was like someone had flicked a switch.

Every person in the bleachers began to look around, not understanding what had occurred.

Pops began to rub his temple, as if he was suffering a migraine.

"What the hell was that?" Baseball Cap asked, his head swiveling back and forth as he tried to discern the abnormality.

Slacks shrugged. "They must be having a problem with the park lights. A power surge or something."

As if that settled it, no one else asked about the strange occurrence, and once more everyone focused their attention on the game.

"Hey," Sweater vest said quietly to Jogging suit. "I gotta pee."

"Again?" Jogging suit said loudly. "You just went during the middle of the third inning.

"Geez? You wanna tell the world?" Sweater vest rebuffed.

"Now coming up to the plate: number 51," the umpire announced again.

"Oh, sweet Jesus," Jogging suit said with dread. "Here we go. Now Milton is coming out of the dugout."

"Number 51?" Pops said, not asking anyone in particular. "But I thought Walker was at bat."

"What's wrong with Milton?" Sweater vest asked her friend.

Jogging suit flashed a knowing smile. "You'll see." The pitcher got into a windup, about to throw a pitch. "Wait for it."

"Strike one!" the umpire yelled, a few boos following the call.

Everyone in the bleachers watched as the batter flung his baseball bat in anger. The bat tumbled end over end until finally coming to a rest.

"Oh, my," Blue jeans said. "That bat sure went quite a distance, didn't it?" She still tried to be supportive. "Nice... uh... throw there, uh, Milton?"

"Yeah," Jogging suit snorted, "if baseball was based solely on bat flinging, Milton would be an MVP."

"Don't worry, Milton! You're doing fine!" Blue jeans called, unperturbed.

"Strike two!" the umpire yelled.

"Oh, dear," Blue jeans sighed.

Sweater vest leaned over and called down to Slacks, who was below her, "Hey you! Does he usually play?"

"No," Slacks replied. "There's no *mandatory play rule* in high school ball.

"What did you just say?" Pops said quickly.

"Yeah," Jogging suit added, "his only sports-related injury was a hemorrhoid from sitting in the dugout for too long."

"Then why is he playing?" Sweater vest asked.

"Just wait for it," Jogging suit said with a wry grin.

"Strike three! You're outta there!" the umpire yelled.

"That's okay, Milton," Blue jeans called out in support. "You'll get him next time!"

"You mean if he's still with the team next time," Slacks said. "From what I hear, Milton hasn't been 'fitting in' too well in the clubhouse."

Pops nodded, recalling something from his past. "Yes, that's true."

"Do we have any sandwiches left?" Jogging suit asked. "I'm starving."

"Are you kidding me? You just ate," Sweater vest said.

"I did?" Jogging suit asked, frustrated. "No I didn't. Just give me a sandwich already."

"Fine, but I still gotta pee," Sweater vest replied and took out another sandwich.

Her friend took it and quickly sank her teeth into it, and with a mouthful of food, waved in the general direction of the bathrooms. "Then go," she said. "You're not a fountain statue. No one's holding you here."

Pops looked confused once more. "High school?" he said to no one in particular. "I thought this was Little League playing today."

"Are you kidding, mister?" Blue jeans asked. "Just look at the size of those guys."

"What inning is it again?" Baseball cap asked, then let out a sickly cough. He looked as if he was coming down with something.

"Bottom of the seventh," Slacks called over to him.

"I have to pee," Sweater vest repeated.

"You've been saying that forever," Jogging suit said, throwing her hands up in annoyance. The sandwich was finished and only a few crumbs remained in her lap.

"I have not," Sweater vest snapped back, frustrated. "I just mentioned it a moment ago."

Jogging suit swiveled in her seat to glare at her friend. "Look, if you have to go, just go already."

"Go where?" Slacks asked, overhearing the conversation.

Sweater vest flushed red, embarrassed that her bodily functions were now being discussed openly. "Nowhere. I'm fine."

"Oh good," Slacks said, "They're changing for the seventh inning."

Pops blinked in surprise upon hearing this. "Seventh? I thought it was the bottom of the sixth?"

"You're confused, Pops," Baseball cap said. "It's not the sixth, it's the *final* inning of the game."

Pops was even more confused than before. But he was nonplussed and he stood taller, as if he was confident in his reply. "I know that. I know it is. It's just..."

Suddenly, the lights flicked out and the field was plunged into darkness. It was almost instantaneous, and if anyone in the bleachers had blinked, they wouldn't have even noticed. But where Pops was, everyone there looked up, as if wondering if a solar eclipse was occurring or some other natural phenomenon.

In the bleachers, Pops rubbed his temple again, as if something inside his head had caused the oddity.

As Baseball cap stared up at the sky, a flash of nervousness crossed his visage. "What the hell was that?" he asked and then glanced at Pops, upon seeing the old man looking distressed. "Hey, Pops, you all right?"

Slacks was scratching the side of his head as he looked all around the field. The game was moving forward as if nothing had happened. "It must be the park lights; has to be a problem with them or something." He opened his notebook and began scribbling in it. "Someone will need to report this. I'll do it after the game."

Baseball cap hadn't taken his eyes off of Pops, and he called out to the old man again. "Did you hear me? I asked if you were okay."

Pops came out of whatever fugue state he was in and gazed over at Baseball cap, then slowly, as if his head was on a rusty hinge, he began to nod. "Uh, yes, I'm fine, thank you for asking."

Slacks finished writing in his notebook and placed it on the bench beside him. "Hey look! A new batter's coming up to the plate now. It's Onakowski. Man, has he had a really great year."

"Now coming up to the plate!" the umpire yelled, "Number 51!"

People began to clap and holler. It was obvious that Onakowski was a fan favorite.

Pops began massaging his temple in confusion. Something wasn't right about this, but he couldn't figure it out. He looked out onto the field then at the people in the far bleachers, then at the fans closest to him. It all wasn't right, but he couldn't put his finger on what was wrong. "I thought 51 already batted?" No one paid him any attention.

"That's Onakowski? Blue jeans asked, as she eyed the batter with curiosity. "What's his batting average?" she called out to Slacks, who seemed to have the stats for all the players. She had seen his type before. Studious on his fact-keeping. In his career in life he was probably an accountant or a financial consultant; someone who liked to work with numbers all day.

Slacks began to talk and then he paused, as if what he was going to say had been on the tip of his tongue and then he'd lost it. He looked down, staring at his feet, unsure of his reply. "You know what? I can't seem to remember."

"Well then, why don't you look at your notebook?" Blue jeans suggested.

Slacks turned to look directly at Blue jeans; he gave her a curious look. "Notebook? What notebook? What're you talking about?"

Blue jeans threw her hands in the air. "You just had it in your hand.

Slacks looked down at his hands, then rubbed his temple, now feeling very unsure of himself."

"Did you put it under your seat?" Baseball cap asked.

Slacks shook his head. "No, I don't think so." He looked around, studying the other benches and people closest to him. "I don't see it. Are you sure I had one?" Maybe it wasn't him that was confused, maybe it was the others.

Pops ignored everything that had just transpired. His attention was focused out on the field. "Wait a second," he said confidently. "Number 51 was Milton..." But then he hesitated, once more unsure of himself. "Wasn't he?"

"Of course I'm sure," Blue jeans said but then reconsidered. "I think I'm sure. Well, never mind. What's his RBI? You know that, at least?"

Slacks shook his head. "Beats me. Why would I know that?"

Blue jeans grew frustrated. "Because you're the guy. The guy who..." She paused, not remembering what she was going to say. "Well, then how about his home run ratio? Do you know that?"

Slacks shrugged. "No, I don't know that either."

Blue jeans frowned. "Then how do you know Onakowski has had a really great year?"

"Because I've seen *Mrs.* Onakowski," Slacks replied. "And considering the amount of bling she wears on a daily basis, he better be doing well."

Jogging suit waved a hand to get Slacks' attention. "Nah, they pay crap in the minors."

Pops blinked and did a double take. He didn't understand any-thing that was happening. Things kept jumping around quicker than he could keep up. "The minors?" But then a moment of clarity struck him and he gazed out onto the field and said, "Wait a second. This game. I remember this game." He'd been sitting down but now he jumped up, filled with more animation than anyone had seen him with upon arriving. "I know this guy's stats. 667. Onakowski. His BA is .667. That's it!"

As Pops began reciting stats from memory, Slacks suddenly joined him, the two speaking simultaneously. "He's eight and twelve, eight hits, five runs, no strikeouts."

Jogging suit stared at the two men for a moment, then said to Sweater vest, "Okay, now that was just too weird."

"You're outta there!" the umpire yelled as the batter was struck out.

The crowd clapped and booed, depending on which team they were rooting for, and Pops and Slacks both sat down.

"Wow. That was amazing, Pops," Baseball cap said.

"What was?" Pops asked, once more looking confused, as if he didn't understand what was going on.

"You called out his stats like you knew it all off the top of your head," Baseball cap said, impressed.

"I did? Well, I…" Pops paused then added, "Knew what?"

Blue jeans leaned down to Slacks, who was rubbing his temple in a similar fashion as Pops had earlier. "You okay?" she asked.

"No," Slacks replied. "My head hurts. I think I need some Ty… Tyle… Ty… something…" He stopped talking and became very still and quiet. "I'll be okay. I just need a minute to get it together."

"Now coming up to bat, number…" the umpire began and then paused, as if he couldn't recall who was about to step onto home plate. "Uh… number…number…"

Sweater vest leaned close to Jogging suit, and whispered, "I really gotta pee."

"Is this still the minors?" Pops asked the people around him. But after no more than a heartbeat said, "Something's going to happen. Something that matters."

Sweater vest was still bugging Jogging suit, who snapped, "Would you stop it already? You've been saying it for hours. Just go if you have to go. No one's stopping you."

"Number 51," the umpire finally said.

"But I don't wanna miss the end of the game," Sweater vest said.

Jogging suit rolled her eyes in annoyance. "Would you rather keel over and die because your bladder burst?"

"Can it really do that?"

"No. Not 51," Pops said, a look of concern crossing his ragged features. "Not again."

Jogging suit let out an exasperated sigh. "For Christ's sake. Just go already."

Sweater vest considered the suggestion, and after a full ten seconds replied, "Nah. I'll wait." Still, she squirmed in her seat, the pressure of her bladder a constant reminder that she needed to pee.

Jogging suit let out another sigh. "Oh, Sweet Jesus."

The sound of a cracked bat filled the air, the baseball hitting the bleachers with a loud thud of hard leather on wood. Every single fan reacted by ducking out of the way, not wanting to get hit by the foul ball. The ball came closest to Baseball cap and Pops.

"Whoa!" Blue jeans yelled excitedly. "That could have killed someone." She cupped her hands around her mouth and called out, "Watch where the hell you're hittin', you stupid jerk!" She blinked as she said it, then shook her head as if to clear it. "Wow. That's not like me at all."

Slacks turned to Pops. "Are you all right there, mister?"

"I'm fine. I'm...okay," Pops said.

"It was like he was aiming for you or something," Jogging suit said.

"No, he wasn't," Pops replied with a shake of his head. "He was trying to impress a girl." A light could be seen in his eyes, as he recalled something, a memory that was deep in his mind. "A pretty girl, actually. Not here though." He pointed over to the right. "It was over there."

Baseball cap followed where Pops was pointing and then, he too, nodded. "Yes, that's right. Her name was Vanessa Martinelli, right?"

Jogging suit began to laugh. "Ha! Like that old guy would ever have a shot with her."

Slacks ignored her taunt and stood taller, defiantly, and with confidence replied, "No, he will. He'll marry her someday. He paid…"

Pops spoke up, butting in, Slacks then going silent. "He paid the pitcher from the opposing team five dollars to write '*Vanessa, will you go out with me?*' on the ball."

Jogging suit was laughing even harder now. "Oh yeah. His plan was to send the ball out there towards her so she'd pick it up and be so impressed with the maneuver that she'd go out with him."

Slacks held up a hand to stop the woman from going further. "But wait a second. He didn't put his name on the ball. So, might not Vanessa have thought it was actually the pitcher who was asking her out? Or even the batter?"

Baseball cap nodded, jumping in. "The batter thought of that, too, just before he swung at the ball. That's why it landed here."

"That's a bad idea," Jogging suit scoffed. "The mother of all bad ideas."

Blue jeans shook her head. "No. Girls are impressed by things like that."

"Says who?" Jogging suit snapped.

Slacks gestured to Pops. "He does. Or he did, anyway. I'm not quite sure."

"I wonder," Pops said. "Did they ever get married?" Then he seemed to pull something from his memory. "Wait a minute.

Martinelli. M… M…" It was coming to him slowly. "Milton. Something happened to Milton."

"You got that right, Pops," Jogging suit laughed.

"I just remembered what it was," Pops said but then he lost it. "No. I guess I didn't."

Blue jeans began nodding. "He hung himself."

Pops shook his head. "No, that's not it."

"What're you talking about?" Jogging suit asked. "He blew his brains out."

Pops began to sway back and forth slowly, as he mourned the loss of Milton. "No, no, no."

Slacks' head suddenly snapped up as he remembered his notebook. "Wait, I did have a notebook. But where is it?" He began searching around him. The notebook was actually right there next to him on the seat but for some reason he couldn't see it.

Sweater vest was still talking about Milton. "Nah. He OD'd on painkillers, I think."

"I thought he jumped out a window because he thought he was Superman or something," Blue jeans suggested.

"Nah," Jogging suit rebutted, "that was George Reeves."

"I thought he was the guy who fell off a horse?" Baseball Cap said.

"I thought that was Chris Reeves?" Blue jeans corrected.

Slacks was still looking for his notebook, crawling around the bleachers with no luck. Then his head popped up. "Chris Reeve."

Blue jeans looked annoyed. "Whatever. I thought he blew his brains out?"

Sweater vest leaned over and bumped Jogging suit to get her attention. "I thought you said that was George Reeves?"

Jogging suit spun in her seat, her face filled with anger. "Who cares? We're talkin' about Milton here!"

Pops looked about ready to cry. "Milton. He…he died."

Baseball Cap nodded. "That's right," he agreed. "He couldn't stand the…" He began to cough, and almost a full minute went by before he'd caught his breath enough to continue. "The abuse he got from the other players and coaches."

Pops nodded as he struggled to remember some more. No one in his section found it odd that they all seemed to be having the same memories, as if they were all one mind. "He…he was a kind, gentle person."

"He was gay," Jogging suit said flatly.

"So?" Sweater vest said, "A lot of players were."

"You mean a lot of players *are*," Blue jeans said.

"So?"

"But he was way more out in the open about it at a time when a lot of guys weren't," Baseball Cap said. "Many of the other players felt threatened. So, after years of abuse, he…"

Pops was crying now, tears running down his pale cheeks. "They found him strung up in the bathroom."

"See?" Blue jeans said smugly. "I told you." She quickly took on a cheerful tone and called out to the others, "Hey, the batter's up. If he makes the goal, we win!"

"Now coming up to bat, number 51!" the umpire yelled.

Slacks still struggled to find his notebook, and he was becoming anxious. "I must remember where it is. I must remember where it is."

Baseball Cap looked behind him at Blue Jeans, a look of confusion crossing his features. "Did you just say 'goal'?" He began to cough, a hoarse cough that forebode the coming of a bad cold. "This isn't football, it's…" He was damned if he could recall what he was about to say.

Suddenly, all the fans in the section with Pops began to fidget, their faces taking on an odd look of confusion. Some seemed more uncomfortable than others though.

"Now serving, number 51!" the umpire yelled.

"Now that doesn't sound right," someone said but who it was didn't matter.

"I gotta pee," Sweater vest whined.

Blue jeans leaned over and got Baseball cap's attention. "What did he say?"

Baseball cap shrugged, not having a clue.

The umpire's voice called out again, "Number 51 has to go pee!"

Jogging suit shoved Sweater vest. "So then go. No one's stopping you."

ANTHONY GIANGREGORIO

Baseball Cap looked more confused than ever. "It's..." Whatever he was trying to recall just wouldn't come, no matter how hard he tried. It was frustrating to the point of madness.

The umpire's voice began to rant, words blurring into more words. "Sesame Street was brought to you today by the number 51 and the letter P!"

Sweater vest twisted in her seat to face Jogging suit. "Come with me. I'm begging you. I don't want to go alone."

Slacks began counting, like he was performing a mental exercise. "One. Two. Three. Three."

"The letter 51 and the number P!" the umpire yelled, obviously as confused as the fans.

"I'm not going with you," Jogging suit said. "It's the last inning."

Slacks kept counting, but as he did, he became increasingly agitated. "Four... five... six... No, wait. Five...five...five...fifty-one... fifty-one..."

"But I forget where it is. The bathrooms, I mean. Please come with me!" Sweater vest pleaded.

Pops stood up from where he was sitting and looked around at the others. "What's wrong with everyone? What's happening?" he asked anxiously.

Sweater vest stood up, went to the end of the bleacher seat she and Jogging suit were on, but no sooner did she reach the end than she returned. It was like she was afraid to leave the bleachers by herself. "Please! I really have to go!" she pleaded again.

38

"You okay there, Pops?" Baseball Cap asked, upon seeing the old man looking confused.

The umpire began screaming, "The letter P! The letter P!"

"So just go if you have to go. But I'm not coming!" Jogging suit yelled at Sweater vest.

"Who's up at bat?" Blue jeans asked.

"Fifty-one… fifty-one… fifty-one…" Slacks repeated over and over.

"But… but… I don't know where the bathrooms are!" Sweater vest cried, almost in tears.

Slacks was chanting, "Three…three…three…"

"The letter P!" the umpire screamed once more. "The letter P!"

"Hey, Pops, you don't look so good," Baseball Cap said, concern on his face.

"Three…three…three…" Slacks chanted.

The umpire was still screaming, his voice blending in with the rest of the fans, who were also either chanting or screaming. "Pee! Pee! Pee!"

Once more darkness descended, blotting out the light. Time seemed to stand still and images began to distort. If reality had been a piece of paper, it was as if a giant hand had begun to crumple it up.

In the blink of an eye it happened again, darkness descending, enveloping everything, and then there was light once more, though the people in the bleachers were still acting strange, and most barely noticed the fluctuation in their reality.

Pops swayed on his feet as the darkness descended and then retreated. "Oh, no. I think…I'm gonna…" He wasn't feeling well at all.

"Just go, damn it! Just go if you gotta pee!" Jogging suit yelled at her friend.

"Go! Go! Go! Go!" Blue jeans began to chant, clapping her hands as she did it. It was like she was cheering.

Pops, standing in the center of the bleachers, suddenly looked down at his crotch, where a wet spot had begun to form, the spot slowly growing. Urine rolled down his legs to pool at his bare feet. For a moment the urine warmed him, but in seconds it became cold, chilling him. He didn't understand why this happened, as it was a beautiful summer day. He looked up, locking gazes with the people watching him, and humiliation filled him to his very core. He'd wet himself, in public, as if he was nothing more than a child who didn't understand the concept of using a bathroom yet.

No sooner did he finish urinating than once more darkness came crashing down, squeezing the life from the very reality Pops was within. No one seemed to notice this time either, as if the light and darkness was nothing to them. All stared at Pops, as if he was the center of their universe.

The umpire had gone silent, and an air of tranquility seemed to suffuse the area.

Jogging suit was the first to speak, and she turned to face Sweater vest and said, "Now look what you went and did?"

Sweater vest looked offended. "Me? What did I do?"

Blue jeans, who had been rather supportive of everyone till now, threw up her hands in exasperation. "That's it, I... I... I can't do this anymore. I have to leave, now." Looking defeated, she pushed past some of the others and left the bleachers, and was soon swallowed up by the darkness that now surrounded the one section of bleachers that Pops occupied.

It was as if Pops and the others were inside a bubble, one where the rest of the world didn't exist, a bubble ensconced in a void of blackness. No one noticed this, however, nor did they so much as glance to the sides or forward, where the baseball field once was.

"Are you all right, Pops?" Baseball Cap asked compassionately.

Pops didn't reply, but stood immobile, staring at his pants as the wetness began to chill him to the bone. The others around him stared also, still in shock at what they had witnessed. It was as if they too were embarrassed and humiliated, though it wasn't them who had soiled themselves.

"You know what?" Jogging suit said, acting as nonchalant as possible, as if what she'd witnessed was already forgotten. "I'm hungry. I sure could eat."

Sweater vest glared at her friend in amazement. "You idiot. You just ate.

"No I didn't. Give me a sandwich."

Sweater vest bent over and checked the cooler, but it was empty. "See? You ate them all. There are no more sandwiches."

Jogging suit frowned. "Fine. Whatever. Listen, this whole thing's practically over, anyway. Let's grab a couple of hotdogs on the way out. She swiveled and glared at Sweater vest. "Well, come on! Let's go!" She waved to Pops. "Nice knowing you, old timer. It's been fun."

Together, the two women gathered their gear and the cooler, and left the bleachers. Soon they were swallowed up by the darkness—though no one else was aware of it.

Slacks let out an excited yell upon finding his notebook. Then he slowly began to walk off the bleachers. As he did, he began tearing the pages out of the notebook while mumbling, "51... 51... 51... 51..." In seconds, he too, was lost in the perpetual darkness that was even now moving closer to the bleachers. The bubble within the ebony flow was shrinking, and no one took notice, or if they did, they didn't care.

Reality was folding in on itself.

Only Pops and Baseball cap remained.

Both men turned to face one another, though neither spoke.

Baseball cap looked seriously ill, as if he was in dire need of a doctor. He began to cough yet again, and when the hacking fit subsided, he sat down, beckoning to Pops to do so as well. "Do you want to sit with me for a bit? There's still a little time left."

"No!" Pops shouted, his eyes filled with anxiousness. "I...can't...sit. I need to walk...to dry off a little." He walked up to the third level of the bleachers, then stopped, turned back around, and said to Baseball cap, "I know what this is now. I know what's happening. I might not know later but for right now, at this precise moment, I know exactly who I am and what's happening to me."

Baseball Cap blinked in surprise. "You do? Oh, good. What a relief. I thought for a moment…"

"No, don't do that," Pops rebutted. "Don't try to be funny. There's nothing funny about this at all. In fact, this is the worst thing I can even possibly imagine happen to someone."

"I'm sorry."

"You're not my son. I thought you were for a second there but now I realize you're not him."

Baseball cap shrugged. "I never said I was. If you thought that, then I'm sincerely…"

"I said stop that!" Pops screamed, his hands curled into fists at his side. "Stop…being…so…so damn pleasant. For this one brief moment of lucidity, at least let me have the dignity of the truth, wet pants and all." He looked out at the darkness, seeing it moving closer. "I know who you are now. I know who the others were, too." He walked down the steps so that he was standing before Baseball cap. "Why did they leave me? Why are you going to leave, too?"

Baseball cap shook his head sadly. "I'm sorry. It's not by choice. See, memories are like the sandwiches the two women had with them."

"You mean that they had too much mayonnaise?"

Baseball cap managed a slight grin at that. "No, not the mayonnaise. Now who's trying to be funny?" He began to cough again, and his complexion grew even paler. "Okay, think of it like this. If shared, they're terrific. But regardless of whether they're shared or not, once they're gone, they're gone."

"Don't you dare try to simplify this," Pops scolded him. "You're not just how I put my shoes on or remember my daughter's name, or my son's. For Christ's sake, you're everything. You're my parents, grandparents, my first home run, my first girlfriend, you're my very essence. In fact, in many ways, you're my very soul."

There was a loud crash of thunder and the darkness moved closer, so that it almost touched the edges of the bleachers. It wouldn't be long now. Reality was ending, and the oblivion waiting beyond would not be denied.

Baseball cap raised his right hand and placed it on Pops' shoulder. "Walker, Onakowski, Milton…"

"Forget about them. What about my wedding day, the birth of my children? My God…my grandkids. You want to take away my grandkids? You want to take away everything that makes me who I am? If you leave like the rest, what makes me special will go with you. That's no way for a man to end his life, hell, that's no way for anyone to…"

"I don't mean to take anything away from you, honest, Pops, none of us does," Baseball cap said and once more began to cough. "But I can't stop it anymore than you can. Look, I'm sick." He let out a heavy breath and sucked in a new one, the sound like a broken locomotive on its last legs. "I'm dying and nothing can change that."

Pops struggled to make sense of it all, while around him, the ever closing bubble of obsidian closed in just a little more. "I'll fight it, that's what I'll do. I won't let this happen to me!"

"You can't stop it. Nothing will stop it; it's like the tides. No matter how much you might want it not to come in, it will in the end. It's inevitable."

"It's cruel is what it is."

Baseball cap nodded. "Yes, it is. And you know what else it is?"

"What?"

Baseball cap coughed again, the sound terrible, like he was about to hack up a lung. He was unstable on his feet and he looked as if he was about to pass out at any moment. "It's biological."

"What the hell does that mean?"

"It means I can't change the way things are." He sighed heavily. "Look, you may have an occasional accident or inconvenience here and there, but let's not forget that I'm still the one who's actually dying here. The others, too."

Pops' jaw dropped open in abject shock. "Accident? Inconvenience? Are you serious? You really just expect me to accept and feel sorry for you? Well, I don't. I don't accept any of this. Go ahead and die then. But do you know what happens next, after

45

you're long out of the picture?" He was becoming furious, his hands clutched in fists again, a large vein bulging on his temple. "I'm still here! You get that?" he screamed. "I'm still here!" Then, like a light switch had been flipped, the anger was gone from his face and his tone took on one of pleading. "Don't you realize what that means for me? You're everything I have, everything that I am." Tears rolled down his cheeks. "You son of a bitch! How am I supposed to go on without you? Or the others? Without you, I'm nothing, just an empty shell where once stood a human being. Do you have any idea how humiliated I feel? Do you have any idea how sometimes, when my daughter comes to visit me at the house or my wife asks me a question, and I look at them and don't even know who they are, that there's absolutely no recognition on my behalf at all, can you imagine how deep down, where there's still a spark of who I am, how I feel? How frustrating it is? It's like being in a mental prison you can never break free from, one where you know eventually you'll simply fade away, like smoke in the wind." He stopped then, his breath coming in fast gasps. Baseball cap had said and done nothing, merely stood and accepted the tirade. Pops was even angrier than before now, as if the younger man's passivity was fueling his rage. "Well, what do you have to say?"

Baseball cap looked like he was on death's door, and it was all he could do to keep standing. "I'm sorry. I...I don't know what else to say to you."

Pops almost jumped back he was so amazed at the reply. "You're sorry? You can't be sorry." He began screaming at the top of his voice. "That's not good enough, damn it! Don't be sorry, just don't leave me! Please, I'm begging you. I need you to stay. You have to stay!"

Baseball cap coughed yet again, and with a hand to steady himself, he gazed into Pops' eyes. "I have to leave you now," he said tenderly and with a hint of ruefulness.

"No, goddamn it. You can't leave me. I'm still here, and without you I'm nothing." Pops' voice was soft, almost a whisper. The darkness was touching the bleachers, only a few feet from both men.

Baseball cap tilted his head in curiosity. "Where are you right now, exactly?"

Pops became excited at the question, and he raised a hand as if to pull an idea from the air. "Ah! I know this. I know this. I... I'm, uh, I..." He wandered around the bleachers for a moment, but no sooner was his clarity in full force, then he could feel it fading. He walked back to Baseball cap while shouting, "I hate you!"

Baseball cap nodded in understanding "I know." It was time, almost to the point of oblivion, when the darkness would absorb everything. He let out a small sigh and slumped to the deck of the bleachers.

Pops went to him and slowly helped the ill man to his feet.

The anger was gone now, and Pops looked at Baseball cap with a kinder gaze. He managed a smile as he thought back to all the glorious memories he'd experienced in his life.

There was the first time he'd met his wife, and how he'd managed to get a foul ball hit in her direction at a baseball game. Oh, how her eyes had lit up upon reading the inscription on the ball.

When she'd turned to face him, he'd been on one knee, holding the small engagement ring he'd saved a month to purchase, and only because of his parents' helping him, was he able to buy it at all. Then there was the birth of his two children. Kimmy and David. Both were grown now. Then later, there were the births of his grandchildren, and the trip to Europe he and his wife had taken five years ago. But though those stood out in his mind, there were so many others. The time he and Vanessa had been walking through the park at sunset. The sun had touched the horizon in just such a way that the entire sky was filled with orange and red.

He'd held her close, and she'd put her head on his shoulder, and then, after making sure they were alone, he'd kissed her. After forty years of marriage, he'd kissed her like they were two young lovers on their first date. So many memories to hold on to, so many things that made life worth living, and now it was all going away, to leave nothing behind but an empty shell.

Tears were in Pops' eyes yet again. "I...loved you all, you know. And I took you all for granted. I never thought you'd leave. I assumed you'd all be with me to the end. You're not supposed to leave me while I'm still alive."

Baseball cap forced a smile "And I loved you, too. We all do, or rather, did." He gathered what strength he had and he held out his arms for Pops, who embraced the younger man as if he was drowning and grasping a thrown life preserver. The darkness had encroached once more and now the two men were the only thing left, the darkness practically touching them. Pops sobbed into the younger man's shoulder, his body wracked with sorrow. Baseball cap tried to separate them but Pops wouldn't let go, as if by sheer force of will he could maintain his hold on the man, and in so doing it, remain in control of his own mind, his own memories. But though he struggled to retain his grip, gently but forcefully Baseball cap separated them. When Pops had gathered himself, he sucked in his chest and stood tall, resembling a man about to be placed in a firing line. Now, at the last second of the loss of his mind, as the very fabric of who he was as a person, was about to be shattered forever, he decided he would try to accept it with at least a little dignity, though in his heart he wanted to rant and rave, to cry and scream, like a toddler pulling a tantrum for a toy he wanted.

Baseball cap smiled wanly and turned to step into the darkness, but before he was fully within it, Pops called, "Wait one more second, please."

Baseball cap stopped and turned slightly so that he could look Pops in the eye.

"Before you go, if you wouldn't mind telling me just one thing, I'd be very much appreciative."

"Yes."

"What's my name?" Pops asked desperately. "For the life of me I can't recall it."

Baseball cap shook his head sadly. "I'm sorry. I can't help you anymore." Without waiting for a reply, he turned and walked into the darkness, the oblivion beyond swallowing him whole.

Pops watched the man go, then sat down as the darkness came closer to him. He knew what the darkness was and it terrified him, but even more, he felt cheated. Of his remaining life, of the years with his wife and family, of everything. To exist without his memories was death, or perhaps it was a fate worse than dying, it was a walking death that he wasn't even aware of.

Pops slumped to the bleachers, his head hanging low. "But it's not fair," he sobbed as the darkness all but touched him. He ignored it, and he raised his head straight up, and though there was no sky, only an inky blackness, he screamed to the heavens. "It's not *fair!* I'm still here! Do you hear me, God? I'm still here! I'm still here! I'm still here!" He was screaming so loudly that his voice cracked. *"I'm still here!"*

The blackness surrounded him so that if he moved even an inch in any direction he would be absorbed by it. He didn't notice. Gathering himself for the second time, his anger quickly became fear, his eyes wide in terror.

"I'm all alone now. They're all gone, I can tell. Where they once were, it's empty now. *I'm alone!*" he screamed in pure terror. In the blink of an eye his composure changed. Now, he resembled a lost and frightened child, his eyes darting back and forth. "I'm scared. I'm scared. I'm so scared." As he began to sob heavily, he laid down on the bleachers and curled up in a ball. He was more like a toddler than an adult. While he sobbed, the darkness enveloped him, and where he thought there would be pain, there was instead nothing, only the void of emptiness of one's own mind.

The battle within Pops' mind was over, and the memories had retreated, the disease the only victor tonight, but though the battle had only been within Pops' mind, he *had* wandered into the cold to end up in the exact same bleachers he had conjured up in his head to make his memories tangible. As he lay there, the bleachers took on an even more dilapidated look. Now that they weren't seen through Pops' fugue state, they were shown for the rundown structure that remained. In fact, the entire field was a remnant of days gone by. The field itself was nothing but a denuded waste- land where here and there scrubs of weeds fought to live. The lines that made up the diamond were long gone, and only the barest hint of the diamond shape could be made out, and this thanks to the local children who sometimes came to mess around. The scoreboard looked as if it had been through a war and hadn't made it through intact. Only a few numbers remained, most having fallen to the ground to rot in the dirt. Weather-beaten, the paint had faded so that the once bright green was now dark and dingy.

As Pops lay sobbing on the bleachers, red and blue flashing lights illuminated the section of the structure where Pops was.

Soon, the sound of a car door opening and closing melded into the noise of the unintelligible sound of a police radio.

A police officer walked up to Pops, and he cautiously studied the sobbing man to see if he was hurt. **MILLBOROUGH POLICE DEPARTMENT** was on the badge on his chest, pinned to his jacket. It was thirty degrees out and as he breathed, the air condensed before him, making him look as if he was blowing smoke.

"Hey, pal," the officer said. "You can't sleep here. This park is off limits at night." When he saw that Pops was a senior citizen, his hardened expression softened a little.

Pops stopped sobbing and looked up at the man with a dazed expression. The officer had a flashlight in his hand and was aiming it at Pops' face. The officer lowered the light a little so Pops could see that the man talking to him was with law enforcement.

Pops only blinked at the man, not saying anything.

"What's your name, sir?" When there was no response the officer added, "You got any I.D.?"

Pops stopped crying and sat up, then wiped his eyes with the back of his arm. He considered the officer's words, his brow creasing heavily. "Yes, I think I do." He began to search his pockets. "Oh no, I guess I don't." He looked down at his bare feet, then up at the officer. "Can I go home now, please? I'm cold."

The officer only nodded quickly, and then seeing that Pops didn't seem to pose a danger, he relaxed his posture slightly. He knew not to entirely let his guard down, as people that appeared to look harmless had proven otherwise in his career, but his gut told him that the old man before him wasn't dangerous—to the officer anyway. By the looks of the old man, he seemed disoriented, and the simple fact that he was out, alone, in the middle of the night, with no shoes or a jacket, was evidence enough for that assumption.

"Sure, buddy, where do you live?" the officer asked, then touched the two-way radio on his shoulder to speak into it. "Unit Six on site. Looks like I got a vagrant. Will update in a second, over."

"Ten-four, Unit Six. Let us know if you need some backup, over," the radio squawked.

Pops was concentrating as hard as he could, trying to recall where he lived. But no matter how he tried, nothing came to him. "I live…I live."

The officer glanced around one more time, wanting to make sure there were no shapes in the darkness. Only the flashlight he held provided illumination; even the moon was hidden by clouds. "Wow, it's freezing out here. Where's your jacket, and your shoes? It's gotta be around thirty degrees. It's not July, you know."

The two-way radio squawked again, the dispatcher informing the officer about a man suffering Alzheimer's who had gotten out of the house and to be on the lookout for him. The dispatcher then proceeded to give a detailed description of the old man.

The officer listened intently, his eyes moving up and down Pops' form. The description matched; he'd found the wandering old man.

The officer touched his two-way radio again and responded, "This is Unit Six. I found the old man. Crisis averted. He's at the Millborough Park bleachers, east side. I'll stay with him until transport arrives, over."

"Ten-four, ETA, five minutes. Over," came the reply.

The officer nodded and re-focused his attention on the old man. "So, mister, just what the hell are you doing out here any-way? You know what time it is?"

"The time?" Pops asked, confused. "No, I, no, I don't know what time it is. Is it time to eat? I could eat something. But I'm so cold." He hugged himself.

Another car pulled up next to the squad car, and the officer saw that the vehicle was civilian. A Honda, if he was correct, given the bad lighting.

A frazzled woman in her thirties got out of the car and began running towards the bleachers. The officer noted that she carried a jacket and shoes in her arms.

"There you are," she said to Pops upon arriving. Now that she was this close, the officer saw she looked even more worried than before when he'd first seen her exit the car. "I've been looking for you for hours. Thank God I called the police when I couldn't find you." She looked at the officer for the first time. "I'm Kimmy, his daughter. Thank you so much for finding him. I'll take care of him from here."

"Sure. That sounds fine with me." He took a step away from the couple and touched his two-way radio. "Dispatch, this is Unit

Six. Cancel transportation for the old man. His daughter's here; she'll take him home, over." He stepped closer to the daughter and asked, "Is he in a nursing home yet?"

Kimmy shook her head. "No. He still lives with my mother." She moved so she was standing right in front of Pops. "Pops? It's me, Kimmy—your daughter."

"Then who's Vanessa? That was the name on the missing person's report," the officer asked.

"That's my mother," Kimmy said as she began to put the jacket and shoes on Pops. "He does this from time to time. He has his good days and bad days, but lately his Alzheimer's has been getting progressively worse. Mom can't care for him anymore so we agreed to put him up at Saint Patrick's Elder Care at the end of the month, but given tonight, we're gonna have to push it up a little."

"So he's living at home still?" the office asked, wanting to clarify.

Kimmy nodded brusquely, her attention only on her father. "Yes, we live over on Elm St."

The officer blinked in surprise. "Elm Street? Why, that's gotta be three miles from here. He walked all that way by himself? Barefoot and without a jacket at three o'clock in the morning?"

Kimmy sighed as she turned to face the officer. "Unfortunately, like I said, it's not the first time he's wandered off. Though I have to admit, this was the worst one yet."

The officer looked around the field once more, his gaze falling on some discarded and empty beer cans peeking out from the far side of the bleachers. "Man, they should tear this place down and put it out of its misery. These bleachers ain't safe. Been rotting away for years. Nobody hangs out here anymore but teenagers looking for a place to drink." The officer looked at Pops again, though he was talking to Kimmy. "Why'd he come here, I wonder?" he mused.

"I think I know," she replied. "See, Pops practically grew up on this field. He used to play in the minors here before they built the new field over on Grove."

"No kidding? Wow, that was a while ago."

"A little over twenty-three years," Kimmy said.

"Well, I used to follow some local baseball. Was your dad any good?"

"Oh sure," Kimmy nodded. "He played on the Red Sox for almost thirteen years. They retired his number just last year. He was number 51." While she was talking, she'd been buttoning up Pops' coat, and now that he was dressed at least, she took a step back and sighed. "There. All better now, Pops?"

Pops didn't reply, only stared off into the distance.

"They retired his number?" Then recognition creased his face and he smiled. "51? Really? You mean he's..." He took a closer look at Pops, as if seeing the old man for the first time tonight. "Oh, yeah! Now I recognize him. Man, he doesn't look anything like I remember him."

Something seemed to leave Kimmy's eyes at the officer's statement, and a great sadness replaced whatever was left. "It's all part of the disease. It does a real number on a person."

The officer gestured to Pops' pants, seeing how they were wet. "Hey, uh, you better be careful with him. It looks like he's had an accident or something."

Kimmy rubbed Pops' shoulder. "We'll get you home and cleaned up real soon, Pops. Did you eat today?"

"What?" Pops asked, his attention focused out into the darkness of the field. He wasn't really with Kimmy or the policeman, but appeared to be somewhere else.

"I asked if you'd eaten anything today."

Pops nodded. "Yes. I think so. I had a... I was eating a sandwich, and it had too much mayonnaise on it."

"When was that?" she asked.

Pops considered her question, and after a few seconds replied, "I don't recall." He frowned then, his composure resembling that of a shamed child. "I...I had an accident. I'm sorry." He looked down at his crotch.

"No-no-no," Kimmy said and helped Pops off the bleachers. "It's all right. It's all right. Come on, Pops. Let's get you home and to bed. Mom's worried sick about you."

"Okay," Pops said, and allowed himself to be led like the child he so resembled. But when they had stepped onto solid ground, he stopped and gently tugged on her arm. She stopped as well and turned towards him.

"Miss?"

"Yes, Pops?" she asked, her face filled with patience for the father she loved.

"Can you tell me something?"

"Sure, Pops, anything. Just name it." She forced a smile. She wanted to get him home and out of his wet pants.

"Do I like... baseball?"

"Yes, Pops," Kimmy replied compassionately. "You like baseball."

Pops took in her words, as if rolling them around in his head for a while. Eventually, just before Kimmy was going to lose patience, he answered, "Good. I'm glad." He glanced back at the bleachers. "Good." He looked at Kimmy. "That's real good."

With Kimmy leading him, she ushered Pops back to her car, gently got him into the vehicle, and then drove away.

The officer watched the car leave, and when the rear taillights had winked out, he prepared to go himself and continue his patrol. But he decided if he was at the field, he would at least give it one more quick walkthrough, wanting to make sure there was nothing else that might require his attention.

It didn't take him long, and with the chill in the air, he was eager to return to the warmth of his squad car. It was as he was passing by the section of bleachers where he'd discovered Pops that he paused for a moment. There was a small object on one of the seats, and though he was in a rush to return to his car, he felt something pulling him to investigate. Besides, if he was quick, he would see what the object was and be back in his car in minutes.

Climbing onto the bleachers, very aware of the way the old wood creaked under his weight, he walked up to where the object lay. Reaching down, he realized it was an old baseball, and he picked it up and held it in his gloved hand.

At first it didn't look any different than a hundred baseballs he'd held over his lifetime, but as he turned it over in his hand, he found that there were some words inscribed on it. With his flashlight illuminating the ball, he tried to read the faded inscription. It only took a few seconds to piece together the words, as some were faded to the point of illegibility. But he'd always been good at Wheel of Fortune, and this was no different.

"Vanessa, will you go out with me?" he said aloud as he filled in the inscription.

He wondered if the old guy, 'number 51,' had dropped it, but then decided it wasn't worth the trouble of finding out. Turning to face the field, he threw the ball out onto the pitcher's mound, imagining that he was the President of the United States and it was the first game of the season. The ball bounced three times, and then rolled across the field to be lost in the darkness.

Climbing off the bleachers, the officer touched his two-way radio to open a channel. "Unit Six, all clear, resuming patrol. Over."

"Ten-four, Six. Over," dispatch replied.

The officer stepped off the bleachers and made his way to his car, and was soon driving away, the exhaust from the squad car billowing gray smoke into the night air.

The ball park was empty once more, only the sound of the wind as it blew through the bleachers to mar the silence.

But sometimes, if someone had been there to hear it, and the wind was blowing just right through the framework of the bleachers, it sounded a lot like a cheering crowd.

101 WAYS TO GET TO HEAVEN

PART 1
JUST ANOTHER MORNING

The morning alarm screeched, the wakeup buzzer loud and shrill, sending Jerry McDonald deeper into the folds of his bed. His hand reached out to hit the snooze button for the third time, but he missed, and ended up knocking the alarm to the floor.

"Damn it," he mumbled into his pillow.

Well, at least now the small speaker was buried in the carpet, and if he really tried, he figured he might be able to squeeze a few more minutes of sleep from the morning sun seeping through the curtains on his windows.

He managed about three minutes before realizing it wasn't going to work out. So with a deep sigh, he decided he might as well get up and join the world.

Besides, he had to be at work in less than an hour, and if he was late again, he would probably get written up by his supervisor.

Kicking the blanket off himself and to the foot of the bed, he sat up and scratched his head. Smacking his lips, he tried to get rid of the foul taste filling his mouth. It tasted like he had chewed shoe leather all night, so Jerry decided the first thing on the morning agenda would be to brush his teeth.

He slid off the bed, but as his right foot came down onto the floor, instead of feeling the soft plushness of carpeting, his foot sank an inch deep into a wet and sticky hairball. But this wasn't a regular hairball, oh, no. This one had about half a bowl of cat food mixed into it, and then just a tuft of wet hair in the center. It seemed that when his cat Fluffy had needed to worf up that small bit of hair, whatever else was in his stomach had come up also. It never failed, too. The cat would always eat a heaping bowl of food before leaving him a present.

With his foot now fully entrenched in the cold spit-up, he sighed and looked for the cat. He just wanted to throw a few imprecations at its face, not that the big fur ball would care.

What a life; to lie around all day and eat and sleep and... well, shit.

Slipping his foot out of the gooey mess, Jerry reached for a tissue and wiped off the slime. Then making sure the rest of his path was clear, he stood up and started over.

The routine in the bathroom went smooth at least, and soon he had made it to the kitchen. He was relishing eating the last donut from the day before. The sweet confection was sitting on his kitchen counter, patiently waiting for him to devour it.

Or so he thought.

Instead of what he wanted, what he got was a half-eaten circle now lying on the floor. Little teeth marks covered the baked good, and it glistened in the morning's rays from too much cat spittle.

"Fluffy, if I get my hands on you!" he screamed to the house.

That damn cat is probably sleeping under the couch or sunning himself in the living room, now content and full of my donut, he thought.

Deciding it wasn't worth finding the cat, he just called into the living room, hoping the animal was in there. "Hope you enjoyed my donut, ya jerk. I hope it gives you worms."

Then realizing the futility of fighting with a dumb animal, he slipped on his coat and left for work. There was a coffee shop on the way there; he'd grab a muffin or something before catching the bus.

On his way out of the kitchen, he saw the note he'd left on his refrigerator. **CALL BROTHER** was written in bold letters so he would remember. Both he and his brother were orphans, but despite all the odds, they had managed to stay together through all the foster care and orphanages. When he had reached eighteen, Jerry had left and never looked back, his brother right behind him.

Still, Jerry always wondered what it would have been like to grow up in a real family, with real parents.

While he walked down the street to the bus stop, thoughts of a blueberry muffin floated into his mind. Without realizing it, he started to smack his lips.

Checking his watch, he realized it was well past eight a.m. He needed to be at work by nine, so he should be fine.

He had ten more minutes before his bus came, so he entered the coffee shop on the corner, looking forward to that blueberry muffin.

"Hi, Jerry, what's up?" Susan asked, the perky young woman who was working the counter this morning.

"Morning, Susan. How's Rick?" he asked, regretting it the moment he said it. He had accidentally opened Pandora's Box. From past conversations with her, Jerry knew she was having some romantic problems with him.

"About the same; he just won't commit. Every time I try to get close, he just pulls away. I try to…"

That's all Jerry heard. After that, he quickly tuned her out for the next two minutes. She was sweet, but she was like a broken record. He wanted to tell her to just dump the guy, but knew that like a lot of other women, she craved the drama, even if it drove her crazy.

He kept nodding and uh-huhing until the appropriate time and then he cut her off. "Look, that's great, Susan, but I'm running late for work so could you just help me, please?"

"What? Oh of course, I'm sorry. What would you like?"

"A blueberry muffin would be great," he said.

Her face went into a pout and she turned to look at the back wall, where all the pastry was supposed to be.

"Oh, I'm so sorry, we're all out of pastry. We got wiped out today."

"Well, what do you have left?"

She turned around and bent down to the bottom rack on the wall. With a piece of wax paper, she picked up a day old cruller and held it under his nose.

"We've got these. They're left over from yesterday. Otherwise they'd be gone, too." She frowned just a little. "They're kind of stale, though."

Jerry was about to give her an answer when he heard the rumbling of an engine, a bus engine, coming from the street outside. He turned around quickly and his heart sank as he watched the number 10 bus driving off. He checked his watch and saw the bus was four minutes early. He knew the bus company had a five minute window and he had just blown it.

"Ah, forget it, Susan, I gotta go, that's my bus," he said, running out of the coffee shop like a marathon sprinter.

Susan waved and then went back to cleaning the counter, Jerry already forgotten.

Jerry hit the shops' door and pushed through it, jarring his arm as he went. The bus had just pulled away and he ran after it, his briefcase flying next to him like he was trying to make it hover on its own accord.

He made sure to get behind the bus, so that the driver could see him, waving frantically and calling for it to stop. For just one brief moment the bus driver's eyes and Jerry's met in the man's side-view mirror. Jerry saw recognition in the man's face, too. The bus driver now knew he had a passenger running behind the bus.

But instead of stopping, the driver stepped on the gas pedal, and the bus surged forward with a burst of oily smoke and a revving of the engine. As Jerry watched the bus pull away, he distinctly caught the driver's face in the mirror for the second time. His mouth fell open when he saw the man was smiling one of those mischievous grins that are best seen on ten-year-olds.

Jerry stopped running and stood in the street, watching his ride to work moving farther away.

With his head down, he started back to the bus stop. He hadn't realized how far he'd run. He had a good seven or eight minutes left of walking until he returned to the closest bus stop. The next bus should be by to the pick up spot within the next ten minutes before it would go into the city, but that few extra minutes would make him late for work.

He started back, walking slowly. Now he would be late for work and get written up. While he walked in the gutter, he paused.

His shoe felt funny.

While leaning against a fire hydrant, he looked down and bent his foot up so he could see it better. As Jerry did this, he was still standing in the gutter of the street. As he examined the bottom of his shoe, he realized that the stitching had come undone and the entire shoe was threatening to fall apart.

"I don't believe this, I just bought these shoes," he mumbled, wondering if his morning could get any worse.

Looking up into the clear blue sky, he sighed.

"What else are you gonna do to me today, God? My pants are still intact, how about splitting them up my butt? Or I got it, how about making it start raining. That would be fun if I showed up at work with one shoe and soaking wet."

He looked back down at his shoe again. Standing in the street with one leg in the air, he struggled to see if there was any hope for saving his fractured footwear.

*   *   *

Two-hundred feet away from where Jerry was standing, focused on his broken shoe, a sweet old woman was driving her car. She was at least eighty, and frankly should have stopped driving when Clinton was in office. But she loved her independence and so continued driving long after her expiration date had passed.

Like a lot of older women who were trying to keep up with the times, she had a cell phone. Her daughter had given it to her on Christmas, figuring that way her mom would always be able to call for help if there was a problem or she was feeling sick

So the little old lady with the coke-bottle eyeglasses, with her head barely peeking over the steering wheel, and her left blinker still on from the turn she'd made about two miles ago, drove down the road.

Her cell phone began to ring.

It was her daughter, checking to see if she was coming to the house for lunch today.

The sweet old lady, who could barely see, turned her head to pick up the cell phone. As the little thing rang, she tried to remember how to answer it, forgetting in her age that all she had to do was open it.

Her attention was fully focused on this one small task, and she didn't realize the nose of the car was drifting into the gutter of the street.

With one hand on the cell phone and one on the steering wheel, her driving chores were all but forgotten as she tried to discern this new marvel of technology called the cell phone.

* * *

Jerry gave up trying to fix his shoe, it was hopeless. The icing on the cake was that they were brand new and he had thrown out the receipt. Normally, if he did something like that, he would just go out in the trash and get his hands dirty, but not this time. His luck was holding this morning and he realized it had been trash pickup today, remembering the barrels having gone out the night before. By the time he returned home in the evening, the barrels would be empty, and probably rolling around halfway down the street for good measure.

With a big sigh, he turned around to return to the bus stop, wondering what else could possibly go wrong today.

As soon as he turned around, he saw a big car coming straight at him. In that split second before impact, time seemed to slow, and he noticed the small tuft of gray hair behind the steering wheel. If there was a head belonging to that hair, he couldn't see it. A bird flew by overhead, seeming to pause in mid-flight. Jerry studied its wings. An ant was sitting on the curb below him, deciding if it should chance the long drop to the street and try for the piece of donut someone had dropped out of their car window in passing an hour ago.

All this was taken in and processed in the blink of an eye. His mind saw what was about to happen and he couldn't help but chuckle. His eyes turned upward and he looked into the sky once again.

"Good one," he said under his breath, and then he was flying over the hood of the car, his legs bending one way, his torso the other. The world went topsy-turvy for the briefest of moments and then there was nothing but darkness.

The old lady became startled by the noise of Jerry's bouncing body and hit the brakes, her car swerving some more and striking the fire hydrant, sending a surge of water into the air. In a second the street was a river, Jerry's shattered body becoming soaked, the small amount of blood from his wounds washed away by the flowing water.

Susan and a few others ran out of the coffee shop to see what had happened, and a man in an overcoat ran over to Jerry's prone and battered form. "Out of the way, I'm a doctor," he screamed, pushing through the street gawkers to reach Jerry's side. The doctor touched two fingers to Jerry's neck, but after seeing the position of the neck and body, he already knew what the result would be.

Standing up, he looked at a few of the faces surrounding him and shook his head.

Susan brought her hands to her mouth and let out a shout of horror. "Oh my God, I was just talking to him," she said as one of the other regular patrons took her by the shoulders and helped her back into the coffee shop.

The sweet little old lady climbed out of the car, the water soaking her to the bone.

She stood there, scratching her wet hair, wondering what had happened and what all the commotion was about.

As for Jerry, he lay in the street, dead. His briefcase floated away on the current of water, his left hand seeming to float next to his body in the pool of water, as if he was trying to hail a cab, still worried about being late for work.

PART 2

SO THIS IS HEAVEN?

Jerry opened his eyes.

Disoriented and feeling a little woozy, he was surprised to see he was in a waiting room. Old magazines littered the small coffee table in front of him and a water dispenser sat quietly in the corner, being ignored.

The strange part was the other people that shared the room with him.

In the rows of chairs lining the wall across from him sat four people, all in a state of undress and dishevelment.

The first was a woman in her mid-forties or early fifties. She was wearing nothing but a towel, and her hair continued to drip water onto her seat. The second individual was a man, late forties if Jerry was correct. He looked like a construction worker, thanks to the brown jacket, jeans, and the heavy work boots that had metal fabricated into the tips.

What was shocking was that the man had what looked like half a brick lodged in the top of his head. What was even stranger was the man barely seemed to notice. He just sat quietly, reading a People magazine and sipping from a small cup of water.

The third individual was a young man in his early twenties. He had the look of a metal head or some kind of punk rocker. He sat quietly with his legs crossed. In the skin of his left arm a needle dangled, complete with the rubber hose tied off at the top. The rest of the arm looked like a bird with sharp claws had run up and down his arm, leaving tracks.

The fourth and last person was a man about Jerry's age. He seemed normal enough with the exception that he was in his pajamas and a bathrobe. Jerry was feeling nervous and so wanted to talk a little, still not understanding where he was.

"Hi there. I'm Jerry, I was wondering if you had any idea where we are?"

The man in the bathrobe turned to look at him, a look of almost-boredom on his face. "Hey there, Jerry, name's Clyde, I'm in computer software. And what do you mean by 'where are we'?"

Jerry leaned a little closer to Clyde and lowered his voice some more. "I mean, I have no idea where I am or what the hell's going on here." He gestured to the construction worker. "That guy has a *brick* in his head."

Clyde casually turned to look at Brick Head. "Yeah, so what else is he supposed to have in his head if not a brick?" Clyde inquired with a smile.

Jerry shook his head back and forth. "No, you don't understand, he has a brick in his head. Shouldn't he be dead, or in a hospital at least?"

Clyde looked at Jerry again, as if seeing him for the first time. "Jerry, old pal. What's the last thing you remember before you came to be here with me in this room?"

Jerry had to think about that one for a moment. He had gotten up for work and had walked to the bus stop where he wanted a muffin, but they were out. The bus had left him and then he had…

It hit him in a rush, the memory flooding back. "Oh my God, I was hit by a car."

Clyde nodded. "There you go, that's right. I have to take your word for it, but it sounds right enough." Clyde pointed to the other people in the waiting room with Jerry and himself. "You see that woman there? She slipped in the bathtub and cracked her head; skull fracture. That guy with the brick? Took off his hardhat on the job and walked under one of his buddies, who was working a few stories up. Brick came loose and the rest is obvious. That kid there? Overdose, if it isn't blatantly obvious." He patted his chest. "I had the misfortune of having a heart attack. Happened in my sleep, never woke up after I went to bed the night before." He tapped his chest over his heart again. "Too many fast food burgers, I guess."

"So I was in a car accident?" Jerry asked, still quite shocked.

Clyde nodded. "You bet. Welcome to the waiting room of the afterlife."

Jerry's mouth fell open and his mind raced. How could this be? He couldn't be dead, it wasn't fair. He had so much to do still, so many places to go, things to do.

He sat in that chair for hours, then days, and then weeks, the others with him. Slowly, as time passed, one by one they were called through the door at the far end of the room. The door would open and a bright light would shine through. Each person would wave goodbye and walk into the light, the door closing after they were gone.

Finally Jerry was alone in the room. He sat there for a long time. How long exactly he had no idea, and slowly, he began to accept what had happened to him.

When he did, at that precise moment, the door opened and bright white light flooded into the waiting room.

"Jerry McDonald, step into the light," a disembodied voice told him from within the light.

On shaking legs, Jerry stood up and moved towards the door. With his pulse pounding in his head, he stepped into the light and the door closed behind him. So this was Heaven, he thought. At least he'd made it.

PART 3

TAKE YOUR PICK

Jerry couldn't see anything. He was blinded by the bright white light in his eyes. From somewhere in front of him a voice said, "That's right, Jerry, keep walking forward. You're almost there…and…stop."

Jerry did as he was told. Waiting, nervous and worried.

The light flashed off, leaving behind little pinpoints of light to swirl around in his vision. They faded slowly, and when he could see clearly once more, Jerry found that he was looking at a man in a three piece suit, sitting behind a glass desk. The man was small in stature, with brown hair parted to the side. He was clean-shaven, with a sharp nose. He was pale, as if he didn't get out in the sun too often.

On the desk was a spotlight, now off and turned away from Jerry's face.

The man noticed Jerry's look of surprise and he chuckled. "Sorry about the light in the face, Mr. McDonald. It's just my little joke. You know, step into the light, and all that." He flashed Jerry a wide grin.

Jerry just stared.

The man had a folder in front of him, and he browsed through it, nodding his head every so often. "So," he said. "Car accident, huh? Tough break."

When Jerry finally found his voice, he asked quietly, "Who are you and what am I doing here?"

The man stood up and walked around the desk to sit on the corner. He looked at Jerry. "You're in luck, Jerry. May I call you Jerry?"

Jerry nodded it was fine.

"Well, Jerry, you might be dead, but if you want, you can get another chance to play the game."

Jerry blinked a few times, trying to let it all sink in. "Excuse me? The game?"

The man nodded. "Sure; the game of life. Didn't you ever play the board game? Listen, Jerry, most of the junk you hear about religion is crap. People say and believe what ever suits their own purposes and agendas. Now according to your file, you're nothing, no actual faith in anything."

Jerry stood a little straighter. "Now hold on there, I have faith. I have faith in myself and my fellow man, as corny as that sounds. I believe we make our own destiny, and that we don't have to wait for some divine being to dole out what's good and bad once we're dead."

The man nodded briskly. "Exactly, that's what I meant. You're an independent thinker. We like that around here, Jerry. You're just what we're looking for?"

Jerry's eyes creased. "And just where exactly is here, anyway?"

The man waved the question away. "Irrelevant, Jerry, totally irrelevant. You can call this Heaven, or limbo, or whatever you feel comfortable with. To tell you the truth, I'm not really here either. I'm more of an ephemeral being. I've just taken this form so you can understand things better."

Jerry nodded slowly. Then his eyes started searching the room and the corners of the walls as if he was searching for something.

"May I ask what you're doing?" the man asked.

"I'm looking for the cameras. This is a practical joke, right? I'm on one of those television shows where you fool the guy and then everyone jumps out and laughs and the guy's humiliated."

The man shook his head slowly. "I'm sorry, Jerry, but this is as real as it gets. Look, I've got a thousand more appointments today, literally, so let's move this along. We're sending you back. You can be any animal you'd like, within reason, of course. Just don't ask to be Paris Hilton's dog or Britney Spears' cat. It can't be done. It just doesn't work that way."

"Right," Jerry said, stretching the word out. "Anything I want? Any animal on the planet."

"Within reason, Jerry, within reason. It has to be one of the higher forms of life, such as a horse or dog. Oh, and birds are fine, too. Cats are a good choice, also. In fact, that's our most popular choice."

Jerry thought back to his last morning on Earth and his ruminations on being a feline; he grinned from ear to ear.

"All right then, I'll take a cat."

The man nodded. "You're sure now. Once we're done here, that's it. No back takes. The contract is solid. Set in stone. Solid as a rock. Ironclad..."

"All right, all right, I get it, Jesus," Jerry said.

The man waved his finger in front of Jerry's face. "Please don't use that name here, we're equal opportunity in this office."

"Fine, whatever. So when does this happen? How long does it take?" Jerry asked, curious.

The man smiled at him. It was the kind of smile a child gives when he's taken the last cookie from the jar, but looks his mother in the face and denies it innocently.

"That's the easy part, Jerry." He snapped his fingers and a trapdoor opened below Jerry's feet.

Before he could even scream, Jerry was falling through the hole. Below him was blackness. He tilted his head upwards to see the small square of light quickly receding as he plummeted downward.

With the sound of a maelstrom in his ears from the passing air and his clothes flapping around him like he'd just jumped out of an airplane, he managed to take in enough air to let out one piercing scream.

He continued falling as he was then enveloped in the blackness, until he was gone.

PART 4
WELCOME BACK!

Jerry's eyes opened just a fraction. All he could see was black.

Something warm and soft was next to him as well as other shapes similar to his own. The smell of mother's milk tempted him and he used his new olfactory senses to seek the warm fluid out.

He began sucking from one of the many nipples his mother had bared for him and his siblings. Contentment suffused him as he filled his small stomach.

Time went by and soon the dark of his vision became small blurs, and as more time passed, he began to see.

His soul was now inside a cat.

He looked down at his gray and white paws and turned to see his fluffy tail. He had an amazing sense of balance now, as if he could walk a tightrope blindfolded.

He had brothers and sisters to play with and a mother who loved him. Things were pretty good, he had to admit. He was just thinking he could get used to this until the third month rolled around.

Suddenly, his brothers and sisters were being taken away to never return. The part of his mind that was still Jerry realized that he and his siblings were being given away to good homes.

When it was his time, he found himself being held up in the air by a pretty woman in her early thirties, who looked back at him and made cooing noises and baby talk.

Before he knew it, he was in a cardboard box and being taken to his new home.

Once he arrived, he immediately explored the new house. It was neat and clean and had many windows for him to lie in and soak up the sun.

Life was good. He thought back to when he had owned his own cat and was pleased to see he was right. Being a cat was pretty damn sweet. He still got to watch television, his new owner always leaving it on when she was around.

Her name was Brenda Stevenson, and she had been married for a little over five years. Her husband, Bill, was a heavy-set man who loved his wife dearly. Every morning, Bill would get up and leave for work at around six. He wouldn't return home until around eight that evening.

Bill was a workaholic, and while he was able to buy Brenda whatever she wanted, he was never around to give her the attention she so sorely craved. About six months after Jerry had arrived in the Stevenson home, things began to become more interesting.

It was around ten in the morning when Jerry heard Brenda talking to someone at the front door. He had jumped down off the couch where he'd been lounging, and he moved to the hallway to hear better.

"So yeah, I lost my job the other day. They said they were downsizing. Stuff like that happens to people everyday," a man's voice said.

"Oh, Kevin, I'm so sorry. That's terrible," Brenda said.

"Thanks, Brenda, that's nice of you, but it's not so bad. I get to collect unemployment insurance for a while. So until then, I guess I can relax and take a little vacation here at home."

Jerry saw Brenda's eyebrows go up just a little at Kevin's last remark.

"Oh, really, you're going to be home a lot now, during the day?"

"Yup, you bet. Maybe I'll write that novel I always said I'd write but never had the time. I've got plenty of it now."

"If you have some free time, do you think you might come over one day and help me fix a few things around the house? Bill works all the time and told me I should just get a handyman, but I don't like the idea of strangers in my house, seeing all my possessions and such."

Kevin gave it some thought, his lip moving a little as he reasoned out the question. "Sure, why not. Just tell me when you want me and I'll come over. You've got my number, right?"

Brenda nodded energetically. "Sure I do, it's probably in my phonebook."

"Okay then, I'll talk to you soon," he said and left.

"Bye," Brenda called after him and closed the door. She saw Jerry sitting on the floor and looked down at him. "What are you looking at?" she asked him.

Jerry just stood up and walked away. The couch was calling him back.

* * *

A few days later, Kevin was at the front door bright and early in the morning. Brenda had called him and he'd quickly accepted. Brenda had him working all over the house. He fixed everything from peeling paint to burnt-out light bulbs. He nailed down the old wooden stairs on the back porch and then fixed the floor molding in the living room.

By the time Kevin was done with most of the chores, he was hungry and tired. The clock read a little past twelve in the afternoon, and Kevin was shocked to see that he'd been working for four hours straight.

He sat down at the kitchen table and Brenda handed him a glass of lemonade.

She was wearing a tight, button-down shirt with just one too many buttons undone. The pair of white shorts she wore led nothing to the imagination.

Ss Kevin's eyes took her in, he was glad of it. She was beautiful.

Brenda sat down next to him and they talked for a while. Jerry lay on the kitchen floor, watching and enjoying the show. As they talked, Brenda inched closer, her cleavage easy for Kevin to see.

He swallowed hard and then drank half his glass of lemonade in one gulp.

"How is it?" she purred.

"It's fine, thank you," he stammered. While he was in no way afraid of a woman's advances, he knew Brenda was married and therefore, off limits. But that wasn't the only reason. Bill had been his friend for years and he would never try anything with his wife.

Brenda leaned a little closer and Kevin could smell her perfume.

"You know, my husband works all the time. He never pays any attention to me," she said, her voice low, her eyelids drooping seductively.

"Oh, really, well I find that hard to believe, Brenda. If I had a beautiful wife like you, I'd give her all the attention she wanted."

She blinked at him, more of a batting of the eyes. "You think I'm beautiful?"

He nodded. "Sure, you're one of the best looking women on the street."

She sat there quietly, biting her lip in thought. Then she stood up, and with a gesture, pointed to the stairs that led to her bedroom on the second floor.

"Kevin, I have one more thing that needs a good fixing. It's upstairs. Just give me a minute and then come up, will you?"

He nodded, and she glided to the stairs and was up them in a flash.

Kevin sat at the kitchen table, tapping his hand on the surface. Could she be talking about what he thought she was talking about?

He shook his head. No, that would be ridiculous. This wasn't some trashy romance novel where the lonely housewife needed some attention from the handsome handyman.

It was impossible and frankly, he wouldn't be that lucky.

It was always the other guy who got the hot housewife.

He realized a few minutes had passed and so stood up, finished off the rest of his lemonade, and went upstairs.

"I'm in here," Brenda called, her voice coming from the room at the end of the small hallway.

With his heart in his throat, Kevin walked to the door and opened it. Brenda was lying on the bed, wearing nothing but a see-through nightie. Her head was propped up on the pillow and her feet were curled up under her body.

She looked beautiful and sexy.

"Come here, handsome, and take care of what really needs to be fixed," she purred softly.

Kevin ran his hand over his chin, rubbing the small stubble there. He was undecided. On the one hand there was a really hot housewife lying partially nude in front of him, just waiting for him to ravish her. But on the other hand Bill had been his best friend for years.

Brenda rolled onto her back, her perfect breasts calling him.

"Oh, the hell with it," he said under his breath. "I can always get more friends."

He jumped into bed with her and they started their first bout of lovemaking.

Jerry sat in the doorway getting an eyeful. This was one of the times he regretted not being human, because Brenda was wild. She did things to Kevin that day that the lucky man had only read about in magazines.

Finally, it was four o' clock, and Kevin got dressed and prepared to leave.

Brenda sat up in bed and kissed him gently. "Same time tomorrow?" she asked sweetly.

Kevin's eyes lit up. This wasn't a one time thing! "Sure, you bet," he said while getting dressed.

Minutes later, he left the house, running down the stairs and out the back door.

Eight o' clock soon came and Bill walked in the front door, tired and grumpy.

Brenda didn't mind. She fed him dinner and then he went up to bed, while she stayed in the living room watching television.

Jerry sat on her lap and kept her company. Only he knew the truth of what was happening and he couldn't say a word to Bill, even if he wanted to.

* * *

The next morning, Bill left for work like always, and just as soon as his car had disappeared at the end of the street, Kevin was already on the move. He slipped in the back door, and before Bill's side of the bed was even cold, he was having sex with the man's wife.

Off and on all day they had sex and just hung around the house. This went on for days and then weeks, until finally they had become so complacent that they barely thought about Bill anymore.

They were in love, and the fact that she was betraying her husband and he was betraying his best friend meant nothing to them. Everything was wonderful. Jerry had something to keep him occupied, too, and the show was always great. Sometimes he would hop up to the foot of the bed and get front row and center.

He knew one thing; Kevin had stamina.

Two months and five days into the affair, the two of them were going at it in the bedroom. They were making so much noise that neither of them heard the front door open.

Bill had come home from work early. He had thought he would take off for half a day and surprise his wife, maybe take her out to dinner. Despite the fact that he worked constantly, it wasn't because he enjoyed it. He actually hated it. But he loved his wife passionately and wanted to give her all the things she deserved.

He tossed his keys onto the table and stopped when he heard a soft thumping sound coming from upstairs. Not knowing what it could be, he moved to the stairs.

"Honey? Is that you? I'm home early, surprise," he called up the stairs.

No one answered.

He started to climb the stairs and then he heard it again. A thumping sound and then what sounded like his wife screaming.

"Oh my God, there's someone in the house. A burglar?" he mumbled to himself.

As fast as he could, he ran to the den closet and retrieved a small black metal box the size of a shoe box.

The container had a push-button combination on its side, and Bill quickly punched in the numbers. It was easy to remember; it was Brenda's birthday.

Opening the box, he pulled his .38 Smith and Wesson revolver from the black- foam mold that perfectly conformed to the weapon. Snapping open the cylinder, he double-checked that it was loaded, then closed it and hurried back to the stairs.

If his wife was in trouble, it was up to him to save her.

Taking the steps two at a time, he stopped at the second floor landing. He saw that the bedroom door was closed and he moved slowly down the hallway, the gun in his hand leading the way.

The sounds of moaning and banging grew more intense, and with a deep breath to prepare for the worst, he turned the doorknob on the bedroom door and opened it with a strong kick. The door flew inward, the knob hitting the plaster wall and putting a hole in it.

His wife sat up in bed, Kevin having to roll off Brenda in the process. Bill just stood transfixed, his eyes wide. He couldn't believe what he was seeing.

"Now, honey, it's not what it looks like," Brenda pleaded from the bed. Her bare breasts shone with sweat, her hair in total disarray.

Kevin covered himself with the sheet, his eyes going wider than Bill's when he saw the gun in his best friend's hand. "Now, buddy, don't do anything hasty," he said with his hands raised before him, as if he could ward off a bullet with the palms of his hands.

Bill only saw red. "Shut up! Both of you, just shut up!"

They did as they were told, too scared to move.

Bill was slowly falling into a rage that he couldn't control. After everything he'd done for her. This is how she repaid him? And with his best friend, no less. Bill snapped, the anger overwhelming him, his sanity falling away. "Fine, you two want to be together? Then you can be together forever!"

Before either of them could do anything but hold up their hands and turn away, Bill shot them both in the chest. The bullets tore apart their hearts and struck main arteries, the two adulterers dying within seconds of each other.

Kevin fell onto Brenda and lay still.

Bill stood still, not understanding what he had just done in his anger. But as time went by and the sun crossed the sky, leaving shadows in the room that crossed the bed and the two dead forms lying there, he slowly came out of his stupor and saw what his own hands had wrought.

He walked over and sat on the bed, looking at his dead wife; grief overwhelmed him. He had killed two people in cold blood; one of them being the love of his life. He looked down at the gun still in his hand, and without giving it very much thought, he let his grief overtake him.

Without hesitation, and with tears in his eyes, he placed the gun in his mouth and pulled the trigger, his body falling over to lie at his wife's feet.

Jerry sat in the hallway, looking at the carnage.

Great, he thought. Now who's going to feed me with everyone dead?

Four days later, Brenda's sister called the police when her sister wouldn't answer the phone and Bill's work didn't understand why he hadn't come in. The police arrived shortly and found the grisly scene.

The house quickly became awash with detectives and crime scene techs, and soon it was decided that it was a murder suicide.

As for Jerry, he wound up at the pound. He was a full grown cat now and no one wanted him. All everyone ever wanted was kittens.

Time passed and poor Jerry reached his time limit at the pound. They had no room for unadoptable animals. Jerry was taken from his cage and brought to the back room. He tried to fight, but they tied his paws.

"Sorry, buddy, but I guess no one wants you," a voice said from above him, the plastic-gloved hand coming closer with a needle.

There was a slight pinch under his fur and then he felt sleepy. His eyes closed and he cursed his luck. To be reincarnated only to be killed a year later.

This really sucks, he thought, drifting back into the void of death. His heart stopped beating and his muscles relaxed.

Then there was only darkness.

PART 5

LET'S TRY THAT AGAIN

Jerry opened his eyes to find himself in the eternal waiting room again. He was alone, the other seats vacant. He had no idea how long he waited this time, as measuring time was irrelevant, but he looked up when the door across the room opened and a bright white light appeared.

"Step into the light, my son," a disembodied voice said in a haunting voice.

Jerry wasn't amused. He stood up and strode straight into the doorway. A moment later he was standing in the office of the man with the three piece suit.

When the man saw Jerry, his eyes lit up and he turned off the spotlight.

"Oh, Jerry, it's only you. I didn't expect you back so soon," he said while pushing the spotlight over to the end of the desk. "Sorry about the light, just having a little fun with the newbies. I wouldn't have bothered if I knew it was you, though."

Jerry sat down without asking. He crossed his arms over his chest and frowned.

Three Piece Suit came around his desk and sat on the corner. "What's the matter, Jerry, feeling down?"

"Well, yeah, a little. I get a chance at a new life and I die in less than a year. They put me to sleep, for God's sake! Do you know how humiliating that was, not to mention painful? Doesn't feel a thing, my ass. That crap they pumped into me hurt like hell!"

Three Piece Suit man nodded, agreeing with everything Jerry said. "Yes, Jerry, I know all about it. We do get satellite up here, although sometimes there's some interference. We even get the Spice channel, but don't tell anyone I told you." He winked casually with his right eye.

Jerry looked at the man like the guy was insane. "What are you talking about? I don't care." Jerry fumed for a few more minutes before calming down. Now that he had gotten it all out, he was starting to feel a little better. "Sorry about that, it's just that dying really pisses me off. So what happens now?"

Three Piece Suit walked back to his chair and sat down. He opened a folder and started flipping through the pages. "Well, it seems from what I have here that we have an opening for a dog or a bird, a parakeet to be exact."

"A parakeet?" Jerry said. "No thank you. I'll take the dog and it better not be one of those ankle biters. I hate those things." He made a face of distaste.

"I assure you it's not one of those, Jerry. It's a German shepherd I believe," Three Piece Suit said with a smile.

Jerry's eyes lit up. "Okay, that sounds great. Thank you so much."

Three Piece Suit put up his hands in a *stop* gesture. "Please, Jerry, I'm just doing my job." He reached out with his right hand and flicked a switch on his desk. "Well, good luck, and I hope it works out better for you this time," he said with a smile.

Jerry was about to answer when the trapdoor opened and his chair tipped forward. He slid out and into the black abyss. This time he was a little calmer, knowing what to expect. He closed his eyes and enjoyed the ride.

He felt himself losing consciousness and he rolled with it, his mind drifting away until he knew no more.

PART 6

IT'S A BRAND NEW DAY

Jerry opened his eyes to find he was a puppy. He was cute and fluffy and everyone who met him said how adorable he was.

He didn't mind. The part of him that was still Jerry liked the compliments. When he was old enough, he was adopted by a skinny black man named Lamar Johnson.

Lamar needed a watch dog to keep an eye on his various business ventures. You see, Lamar was an entrepreneur.

At the present moment, Lamar had ventured into the profitable world of bootlegging movies. His cousin Jerome would sneak into the movie theatre with a small digital camcorder and tape whatever movie was playing. Then he would bring the copy back to Lamar, who would burn it to a DVD disc and then start burning them on his computer.

At the moment, Lamar was smalltime, only having one computer and one burner. It would take him all day and all night, having to get up off the couch where he'd fallen asleep and change the burnt disc for a blank one.

It was hard work, probably harder than most people thought. He had to burn the discs and write the name of the movie on every one of the covers—the long titles being the worst—then he had to make a copy of some picture of the movie that he'd found from a magazine so his customers would know what movie was what.

Then every disc had to be put into a white sleeve to protect it.

But he wasn't done yet. He still had to inventory everything he had so he would make sure he had enough of whatever was popular for the week.

While he did all this, Jerry would sit on the rug near him and watch him work till the wee hours of the morning. Lamar was usually exhausted when he was finished. For the thousandth time Lamar wondered why he just didn't sell drugs like the rest of his friends. They made more money and got to sleep at night.

Lamar figured he may have been breaking some copyright laws, but he felt he worked damn hard for his money. And who the hell was he really hurting anyway?

What, some Hollywood star might make a little less on a movie and could only afford to buy one Hummer and one Porsche instead of two.

Boo-hoo. Lamar could barely make enough to pay the rent for his tiny, one-bedroom apartment, and hopefully have enough left over for his car insurance.

Lamar packed up all the movies in two small boxes and put all his ruminations behind him.

It was morning and it was time to get to work.

He left his apartment, taking Jerry with him, and packed all his movies into his beat-up Dodge Caravan. The van had ripped window tint on all the windows and more dents than should be allowed on one vehicle at a time. The driver's door had to be pushed in at the hinges before he could open it at all. One of the back windows was gone, replaced by some cardboard and duct tape.

Yes, sir, he was livin' the dream, he was.

Starting the van, it wined in protest for a second before it gave in and started.

He pulled out of his parking spot with a loud screeching of a bad alternator belt, and drove off to his first destination. He did most of his business with body shops and a few car dealerships on the auto mile.

Most of the people he dealt with were just blue collar guys, mechanics mostly.

They were in the same boat he was, except they had a real job where his was a little more improvised. Jerry sat in the front seat with Lamar, enjoying the wind in his face. Lamar would leave the van to visit with each customer. Some bought a few movies and some bought nothing. No matter what he sold, he was still subject to a customer's whims. It was still supply and demand.

But Lamar returned home that night with a few bucks in his hand, still feeling good about his day. He put the money he made into buying another computer, this way he cut his work time in half. He made some more money and he bought a machine that would let him copy eight discs at once.

Now he was able to make all he needed in a few hours, and that gave him more time to see more people and hopefully, sell more movies. Lamar was doing great. His cousin was getting him all the new movies and he had to admit they looked pretty good. He continued to get bigger and bigger and Jerry watched it all from right in the center.

There was only one problem that Lamar had been ignoring. According to the law, he was still breaking the rules. Despite how hard he was working and how well he was doing, he forgot one very important thing.

Jealousy.

His cousin Jerome saw how much Lamar was making every-day and he decided he wanted it all for himself. Jerome picked up the phone one day and made a quick call to the MPAA. The Motion Picture Association of America.

The next day Lamar had some visitors. They barged into his apartment and seized all his computers and equipment. They took him away, as well, and he had to spend the night in jail.

The next day he posted bail and returned home to find his apartment stripped of everything he had worked so hard to build. After that Lamar had no choice but to go into the drug business. He had to eat and he had to live, and he had no other marketable skills.

He actually made more money in the drug game than he ever had making movies, and it was easier. But Lamar wasn't happy, and it was just a matter of time before he started to sample his own supply to try and take some of his own pain and sadness away.

He also found out that Jerome had started up his own little bootleg business, and was now seeing all of Lamar's old customers. Lamar had been betrayed by his own family, even if it was just his cousin.

After that Lamar was shooting up everyday until the end result finally happened.

He received a bad supply and ended up overdosing.

Jerry sat on the floor and watched Lamar in his death throes. There was nothing he could do. He tried licking his master's face and pulling on his shirt to wake him up, but it was too late.

Lamar died, overdosed on his own supply.

Jerry had been a dog for almost two years, the time passing in the blink of an eye. Now Jerry found himself in the apartment of a dead man. The other apartments around Lamar's were empty, only the very poor mixed in with some illegal immigrants living there. The immigrants could hear a bomb go off in the apartment next door and they would keep quiet, not wanting to call attention to themselves and wind up being discovered by the INS.

Jerry had no food and soon had drunk all the water from the toilet.

Days went by and Jerry started to feel tired as starvation set in. There was no food in the house and he wouldn't eat his master. By the time he might have changed his mind, poor Lamar was nothing but rotten meat, his corpse bloated from internal gas.

Jerry howled day and night, but there was no one to hear or the other drug addicts in the building didn't care, they themselves in their own world of misery.

Outside the apartment's windows, people walked by on the sidewalk, unaware of what was happening only a few yards away.

Jerry laid his head down on the floor and whimpered. He had not had food or water for almost a week, and his bones could be seen through his now dull fur coat.

He couldn't believe it was happening again. He was going to die, and this time it was a hell of a lot more painful than just being put to sleep with a shot—and that hadn't been a picnic either!

With one more gasp of breath, he slid into death, joining his master at last.

More than a week passed before someone complained about the smell and kicked in the door to find two desiccated corpses, one human, the other a dog.

The story of Lamar Johnson was over before it had truly started.

PART 7

WELCOME BACK, AGAIN

Jerry opened his eyes to find himself in the waiting room again, but this time he wasn't alone. There were two other people occupying the room with him. One was a middle-aged woman with a bottle of sleeping pills in her hand. Her other hand still held the suicide note she had written before killing herself.

The other was a young man; a teenager really. He had half his skull bashed in. He sat quietly with a skateboard on his lap.

Jerry watched the kid for a few minutes. He couldn't help but comment, "Hey, kid," he said to the teenager. "Bet you wished you'd worn a helmet now, huh?"

The teenager merely made a rude face, then turned the other way.

Jerry grinned at that. The stupidity of being young. It was a damn shame this one kid would never grow up to realize the folly of his youth.

The door opened on the other side of the room and the white light shone into the waiting room. Jerry was ready for this, and as soon as the door opened, he stood up, and walked into the office like he owned the place.

Three Piece Suit's eyes lit up when he saw who had walked into his office, and the man stood up to greet Jerry.

"Jerry, it's so nice to see you again. I…"

Jerry put up his hand for the man to stop talking and he bullied forward with his tirade. "Save it, pal. I'm not interested in your niceties. I'd just like to know what exactly I did to deserve this kind of punishment. I mean, I never killed ants with a magnifying glass when I was in elementary school and I never went around kicking dogs when I was in high school. I'd just like to know why exactly you're making me suffer like this."

Three Piece Suit seemed to stutter for just a moment as he tried to get an answer together. To stall further, he sat down behind his desk and began rummaging through some folders.

Jerry stood in front of the man's desk, his arms folded with a stare that could cut stone.

Finally Three Piece Suit closed the folder he'd been perusing and cleared his throat. "I don't really know what to tell you, Jerry. Usually we have a one hundred percent soul placement. The fact that you're standing in front of me simply defies the odds."

Jerry's frown actually went into an even deeper frown. "Then send me to Vegas so I can do some gambling, because right now

I'd like to see if I can get away with kicking your butt all over this room."

Three Piece Suit held up his hands in defense. "Now, now, there's no reason for violence. I have an immediate opening for you. Do you accept it?"

Jerry's face changed from a frown to a grimace. "That depends; where's my soul going now exactly?"

"That's a surprise; bye now," Three Piece Suit said, and with a wry grin, he pressed the button for the trapdoor.

The floor dropped away and Jerry felt himself falling. He barely noticed this time. He just closed his eyes and waited for the ride to end, his arms crossed over his chest the entire time.

PART 8

YOU'RE SO TWEET

Jerry opened his eyes to find his soul was now in a parakeet. After the first round of humiliation, he'd gradually learned to accept his new place in life. A little old lady named Millie had bought him from the pet store.

She took him home and had placed him in a tiny cage situated in the living room.

For the first few months things had gone pretty well. His cage gave him a good view of the television and he would watch Millie's soap operas with her everyday.

In fact, he couldn't wait until next week when Helen's twin sister Sally was supposed to return from the hospital where she had been in a coma for three months and still had amnesia, but now didn't realize that Helen had stolen her husband while she was asleep.

He still couldn't believe how fast he had become hooked on those daytime soaps.

The next month had gone well, too. That is until old Millie started to feel the onset of Alzheimer's. While it was tough for her, it was even tougher on poor Jerry.

You see, the poor old woman kept forgetting about him, literally, and Jerry was slowly starving to death. He hadn't had a fill-up on his water bottle for more than a week and he was circling down the drain fast. He managed to hold out for yet one more day, but finally succumbed to dehydration and lack of food.

Jerry finally fell off his perch, and with his small legs sticking up in the air, became still.

He would have liked to think Millie would miss him, but the truth was, the old bat didn't even remember him anymore.

His small eyes closed for the last time and he was off to the eternal waiting room once again.

PART 9

LET'S MAKE A DEAL

Jerry opened his eyes and guess where he was? In fact, he had made this round trip so fast that Skateboard Kid and Suicide Woman were both still in their chairs, not having been called yet.

Jerry was fuming. He planned to march into Three Piece Suit's office and kick his butt all over the place.

After an undefined amount of time had passed, the door across the waiting room opened. The same white light poured out and Suicide Woman stood up, preparing to go in.

Jerry beat her to it. "Sorry, honey, but I'm next. Me and him have some unfinished business to attend to." Without waiting for a reply, Jerry charged into the room.

Three Piece Suit stood up and backed away from his desk, upon seeing Jerry storm into his office with clenched fists and jaw taut. "Now, wait a second, Jerry, I can explain. Just let me send you back one more time. I promise you'll be pleased."

Jerry shook his head back and forth vehemently and started to chase Three Piece suit around the office.

"No way, that's it for me. Just send me to Hell or limbo or wherever souls go, because I'm tired of playing your sick game. What kind of entity are you to keep sending me back, only to have me die in a year or so? And guess what? I remember every second of every death. Give me one good reason why I don't mop the floor with you and kick your butt to boot?"

"Well, for one thing, I don't really have a butt. Remember, this form is just for your benefit," Three Piece Suit said matter-of-factly.

That statement made Jerry hesitate for a moment. He had forgotten that despite present appearances, the man in front of him wasn't really a man. He was some kind of angel or something like that.

That made Jerry calm down just a little and he stopped chasing him around the room. "Oh, yeah, guess I kind of forgot about that. But it still doesn't change that what you're doing to me has to stop. I want out," Jerry said and crossed his arms to make his point.

Three Piece Suit moved back to his desk and sat down. "Look, just do one more and I promise you'll be satisfied."

Jerry's left eyebrow went up just a hair, showing his curiosity. "Really? You promise. No more screw ups."

Three Piece Suit nodded quickly, reminding Jerry of one of those toys some people put in the back windshields of their cars. The ones with the bobble heads.

"Yes, Jerry, I promise." He quickly pressed the trapdoor button, but this time Jerry was ready and jumped into the air.

When he came down, his feet landed on both sides of the opening. "Not this time, buddy," Jerry said, giving him a look as hard as stone. "I'll go, but I'm warning you. If it doesn't work out, you better send me somewhere else, because this is it for me. Got it?"

Three Piece Suit leaned back in his chair and smiled. "Relax, Jerry. I'm a professional. This time will be for keeps."

Placated for now, Jerry nodded. "All right then. Wish me luck, will ya. Because the way things are going, I'm gonna need it." Then he stepped out over empty air and let himself drop into the trapdoor.

Jerry fell, disappearing from view and the trapdoor snapped shut with a soft hiss.

Three Piece Suit grinned at his empty office. "Don't you worry, Jerry. This time will be the right one."

PART 10
Welcome Home

Jerry opened his eyes, but instead of seeing light, it was still dark. He started to panic, but realized it would get him nowhere, so he calmed down a little. Still, wherever he had arrived, it was dark and cramped.

There was almost no sound, but sometimes he thought he could hear someone saying something to him. He began to wonder if maybe Three Piece Suit had screwed him and sent him to limbo after all. Where he was now had almost no sensation and he was all alone. He couldn't imagine a worse place to spend forever.

He made due trying to keep himself occupied, thinking of things from his past and what his future might hold. That usually didn't take too long, because at the moment, things were moving pretty slow. At least he never felt hungry or cold; he was thankful for that, anyway.

Time went by slowly and his limbo became even more cramped, until he felt he would end up being crushed by the walls of his prison. When he thought it would become so unbearable he couldn't take it anymore, he found his world collapsing in on itself.

Like an earthquake, his prison heaved and threw him about. He felt himself moving and he went with it, not strong enough to fight.

Suddenly, a bright light hit him in his eyes and he wondered if he was back in the eternal waiting room again. Then he felt a pain where his butt should be and he let out a scream, his new lungs working for the first time.

He blinked up at a man in a white mask and was passed from hand to hand until he was finally cleaned and wrapped in a blanket. Then he was handed over to a woman lying in a bed. She looked down at him and smiled.

Her smile was captivating, and Jerry had already decided she was the most beautiful woman in the world.

Then he felt another consciousness with his and for some reason he knew it was okay to take a back seat and let this other consciousness take the steering wheel.

He knew he would always be in the backseat, but he would make sure the consciousness was always steering them both in the right direction.

For the first time in as long as he could remember Jerry was at peace.

He looked up at the woman's face, and just before he let go for good, to be absorbed into the other consciousness, he heard the woman say something to him.

"Hello there," she whispered. "I'm your mommy and I love you so much. I want you to know right now that I'll love you and protect you with every fiber of my being. No one will ever hurt you."

Jerry heard it all and somewhere deep inside what was left of his soul, he knew it was the truth. He knew he was finally safe and would be happy, for as many years as God or whoever was out there would give this newfound life.

A man walked over to the woman and looked down at him. Jerry thought the man looked familiar but couldn't put his finger on it.

"So what are we going to name him?" the man asked.

The woman's smile grew wider as she stared down at Jerry. "Let's name him after your brother, in his honor. That way we'll always remember him," she said sweetly.

"Okay honey, that would be great," he said.

Jerry's new mother moved him to her face and kissed him gently on the forehead.

"Welcome to the family, Jerry, we're so glad you finally arrived," she said.

Inside, Jerry smiled back at her, agreeing with her sentiments.

He was finally home and the feeling was indescribable. He closed his soul's eyes deep inside the new baby and let himself float into the other consciousness. He knew he wasn't going away, only joining with the other half to make a whole.

That was fine with him.

He had finally found his Heaven.

IT'S FOR YOU

With a limp to his stroll, Walter Whitaker walked up the pathway to his two-family home in Quincy, Massachusetts.

He had lived in his home for almost forty years, and always found himself chuckling at the length of time it now took him to cross the distance from the street to his front door.

He was in his late eighties, his bones tired and weak from carrying him around for such a long time. Still, he was a happy man, glad for every day he had lived on God's green Earth, and hopefully, for many more days to come.

Just before he reached the front door, it opened and out popped his tenant. She was a pretty thing in her early twenties, and Walter sighed when she smiled at him.

In her smile was compassion for a sweet old man, despite the fact that Walter still felt like he was twenty-five in his head, though the arthritis and back pain that plagued his fragile form every day of his existence reminded him he wasn't.

He remembered a time when he was young and healthy, and sweet things like her gazed at him with a different look in their eyes.

"Good morning, Walter. How are you doing today?" Susan asked as she opened the door wider for him. It was well past eight at night and the sun had set hours ago.

"Fine, fine, dear, thank you for asking. A little sore, but I won't bore you with my troubles."

Her smile grew larger. "Oh, it's no trouble. You know that. How's Evelyn doing?"

"My wife? Oh, she's fine. She should be waiting for me upstairs. I stayed out a little late tonight, having a good time with the fellas at the VFW."

She stepped to the side to let him pass and he entered the small foyer of his house. To the right was Susan's door, which led to her first-floor apartment, and to the left was his door, which opened on a set of stairs that would bring him to his own place of residence, the top two floors of the house.

Every day it became harder to climb those stairs, but he had managed so far and figured he would end up dying on those stairs of a heart attack one day.

His wife, Evelyn, had been having trouble with the stairs also, as of late, the seventeen steps that led to the kitchen causing her more and more problems each day. She had been pestering him lately about selling their house and finding something smaller. Something that was easier to clean and navigate with only one floor.

He had laughed at her, telling her he would die in this house before he ever sold it. Years of his sweat and tears had been poured into the walls and floors of the house. Countless items had been changed or added to so he could live in a house that was beautiful as well as functional.

No, he would rather die than give up his house.

Susan stepped out of the foyer and began walking down to the street, where her parked car was waiting for her. "Oh, I see. Well, please give her my best when you get upstairs," she said with a wave. "I haven't heard a peep out of her all day. No walking around, not even the television was on, which was kind of weird." She checked her watch. "Oh, I'm late. I'm going out with a few girlfriends tonight. I'll see you later."

Walter used his cane as a way of saying goodbye, waving it in the air in front of him. As Susan moved off into the night, he turned and slid his key into the lock of his door. Opening it, he stepped into the stairway, and after flicking on the light, began his trek up the stairs.

When he was halfway up them, and pausing for a much needed rest, he called up to Evelyn, hoping she would hear him, but when he received no reply, his lips creased into a frown. "Evelyn? Are you there?"

That was odd, he thought. He knew she hadn't gone out today and even if she had, she would have been home well before dark. Evelyn didn't have the same vision she once had and found it difficult to see in the dark, especially outside where there were conflicting lights, such as headlights and flashing signs.

Not knowing why, his heart skipped a beat and he began climbing the stairs once more. His knees protested and his breath grew short, but he persevered, wanting to reach the main floor and see where his wife was.

With a final lifting of his right leg—minutes later—he stepped onto the landing of his home. Above him were the bedrooms, on the third floor, and he made a silent prayer that he wouldn't have to climb them in his inspection of the house.

While he slowly moved his aging frame down the hallway to the kitchen, he thought back to a discussion he had shared with Evelyn a few days ago. She had wanted him to entertain the idea of getting one of those chairs that attached to the wall so he could ride up the stairs every day instead of climbing them. But stubborn till the end, he denied her petition, stating when he couldn't walk up the stairs on his own two feet, that it would be time for the grave.

She had crossed her arms over her chest and pouted at him in such a way that she reminded him of the young, twenty-something beauty he had fell in love with all those years ago. Not wanting to upset her, he had deftly changed the subject, causing her to forget about the electric chair.

Now, as he walked down the hallway, the kitchen only a few feet away, he absently gazed at the pictures on the wall.

There was their trip to the White Mountains from twenty years ago. Evelyn had been wearing a yellow sundress that made her legs look absolutely fabulous, the dress complimenting her bosom to the point he could barely wait to get her back to their hotel room. He smiled to himself, remembering the night they had spent in the hotel room, making love for hours on end.

The sexual part of their marriage had ended years ago, but not their love for one another. In fact, he loved her more now than he ever had all those years ago when they both had smooth skin and taut muscles.

Upon reaching the kitchen, he noticed steam in the air and began wondering if perhaps she was in the bathroom and had forgotten to turn off a pot of water. But when he turned the corner from the hallway and stepped fully into the kitchen, he realized that wasn't the case.

Evelyn was lying on the kitchen floor, her arms curled into her body like she had been in pain. Her eyes were open, gazing up at the ceiling, as if she was counting all the cracks that had appeared over the years, Walter now to frail to fix them.

"Evelyn! Oh my God, no!" he screamed, and on arthritic knees, leaned down and picked her up, cradling her to his chest. Her eyes stared up and past him and he knew without a doubt she was dead. That was when the tears came, the racking sobs of grief following soon after.

His vision grew clouded as he sobbed with the love of his life in his arms, and when he settled her to the floor, his foot kicked a bottle of pills. With a shaking hand he reached out and picked them up, seeing it was Evelyn's heart medication.

Evidently, something had happened so fast that she had never gotten the chance to open the bottle.

The pan of hot water still roiled and bubbled on the stove, the steam collecting on the ceiling to become water droplets primed to fall. It must have been boiling for hours and the water was all but gone.

Turning off the stove, he pulled his wife to him, squeezing so hard his arms ached as he cried tears of loss and grief.

Above him, the ceiling dripped tears as well, as if the structure itself was mourning the loss of his one and only.

* * *

The funeral was three days later.

There were many people there to say their goodbyes to his wife, but he barely saw them, too lost in his grief to think straight, let alone play the host.

The priest droned on about her immortal soul finally being at rest and how they could all look forward to the eternal rest Evelyn now enjoyed.

He thought it was all horseshit. His wife was gone and he knew damn well she wasn't resting. If she was up in Heaven right now, she would be filled with an angst all her own, filled with guilt at how she had deserted him without so much as a goodbye.

Now he was alone in the world. He had no children to help him get through his sorrow or keep him company, and most of the people he called his friends were two-faced bastards that were only really his friends when they needed something from him.

No, he was alone now; in a quiet world of one.

After the funeral, he informed the priest to send everyone to the VFW. He had rented the hall in the back of the building. It was there so the mourners could get their reward for having to sit through a sermon and drive to the cemetery. At the VFW, they could eat their fill and tell themselves that at least they'd gotten a free meal out of the deal, then they would say their platitudes and go home.

At least until it was his turn.

Vultures, all of them, Walter thought as he turned and left the hall, letting the guests do as they liked.

Climbing into the limousine waiting for him, he had told the driver to take him home, where he planned on getting good and drunk, despite his doctor's repeated warnings of consuming alcohol. He figured he had the right today of all days.

That was just what he did, too. After climbing the stairs to his home, knees aching the entire time, he had pulled out a bottle of bourbon and had gotten good and drunk, finally passing out in his easy chair with his wedding picture in his lap.

As he drifted off into an alcohol-induced sleep, he could have sworn the eyes of his wife in the wedding picture were crying for him.

Or perhaps it was just his own tears splashing onto the glass covering the picture, the tears then running over her smiling face and washing away what was left of his future.

* * *

It was on the one year anniversary of Evelyn's death when the ringing first began.

It was a little past three in the morning, and he had just drifted off into a restless sleep. He didn't sleep well anymore, not since Evelyn had left him.

Now, when he went to bed, the mattress felt like a massive island where he was the only occupant. He missed the smell of her hair, the peach aroma of her shampoo, and the smell of the baby powder she would often douse herself with after a shower.

As he lay sleeping, his hands twitched spasmodically, his mind already falling into a tumultuous dream where he was the only man alive in the world, and he had to live the remainder of his life devoid of human contact.

At the moment, the recurring dream had him walking down a lonely street, the tall buildings reaching up to the sky, the shadows covering everything like a carpet of darkness, always creeping closer as the sun crawled toward the horizon.

When he walked by a pay phone, he was startled when it began to ring. He stood perfectly still, staring at the phone, wondering who could be on the opposite end in the dead world he now inhabited, when the phone stopped ringing.

That was when he went into action, lunging for the phone and picking up the receiver. "Hello, hello, is anyone there?" he panted into the receiver, desperate for a waiting voice that would talk to him on the other end.

But there was nothing. Dead silence. No dial tone, no voice, nothing but dead air.

He placed the receiver back on its hook out of habit, and as he did so, he saw the strong young hand that held the receiver. Only inside his dreams was he no longer a man in his eighties, weak and frail. In his dreams, he was young and strong, a man in his thirties, or perhaps maybe late twenties.

In his dreams his arthritis was gone and he could run for miles without shortness of breath, where the simplistic act such as picking up the phone was not an experiment in arthritic pain.

With the phone forgotten, he stepped away from it and wandered back into the lonely street, searching for someone, anyone, who might still be with him in the city, perhaps hiding somewhere in one of the shadow-filled buildings that stared at him accusingly as he passed by them.

He wandered until the city was behind him, the buildings then resembling modern caricatures of mountains. With nothing but trees and grass surrounding him now, he was startled again when a phone began ringing. Looking around frantically for its source, he couldn't find one.

Still the ringing persisted, and he spun in circles, hoping to spot the origin of the sound.

"Where are you, damn it, where are you coming from?" he yelled to the trees, disturbing birds from their perches in the limbs overhead.

But the ringing didn't stop, and instead grew in intensity until he fell to his knees and covered his ears, trying to smother the annoying sound.

Stirring in his bed, he snapped awake, his eyes gazing up at the dark ceiling. Before he realized what he was doing, he reached out to feel for Evelyn, and for just a fraction of a second, he was surprised not to find her next to him.

Then reality flooded back and he remembered he was alone in bed and would be until the day he died.

He opened his eyes wider when he realized he could still hear the ringing echoing inside his head, despite the fleeting memories of his dream already drifting back from whence they came.

In the darkness of the room, he reached out and picked up the phone on the bedside table. It was over twenty years old, an old Bell telephone, with a rotary dial.

Computers, cell phones, microchips, bah! He was not one to embrace technology, in fact, he rebelled against it. Things were better when he was a child, simpler, back when people had to see one another if they had information to pass on, not like the world now with their impersonal e-mails and text messaging.

His hand fumbled for a minute, searching in the darkness until it rested on the phone. Picking up the receiver, he placed it to his ear, the cold plastic giving him a chill.

"Hello?" he said hoarsely from sleep.

No one answered, and that was when he heard the dial tone, signifying there had never been anyone on the line to begin with. But if no one had called, why was the ringing still in his head?

With a fumbling hand he hung up the phone and sat up in the darkness of his bedroom.

Ring, ring, ring!

It had only been a few minutes, but he was already becoming aggravated.

Ring, ring, ring!

He squeezed his eyes closed so tightly that he saw spots, and buried his head into the pillow, trying to stop the infernal ringing, but it continued.

Ring, ring, ring!

"Stop it, for God's sake! For the love of all that's holy, stop it!" he screamed to the empty room, and all at once, silence descended on him.

He looked around the room, his eyes wide.

Heavy breathing filled his ears, and at first he thought he was imagining it, but as the seconds crawled by and silence reigned once more, he slowly regained his composure.

Sliding out of bed, Walter slowly crept across the carpet and into the bathroom, splashing water on his face to make sure he was awake. In the glow of the small nightlight in the hallway, he stared at his gaunt face. It was times like this when he was most shocked to see himself. In his mind's eye, he always thought of himself as young, perhaps in his thirties or forties like in his dreams, but the face staring back at him was of an old man. Wrinkles, loss of hair, and a drawn face, all gazing back at him without apology or condemnation.

This was who he was now. He was an old man, all alone, with a dead wife, who had been interred in the ground for exactly one year tonight.

His bladder had always been one of weakness, so he peed and had himself a drink of water; though not too much or he would be up in another hour, draining it off.

When he was feeling slightly better, he walked back into the bedroom and lay back down on the bed. His eyes were wide open as he stared at the darkness circling overhead. A car drove by outside the window, the dagger-like lines of its headlights cutting through the thin curtains of the room to play across the wall, until they vanished into the night.

As the minutes slowly ticked by, his breathing calmed and his mind slowly came to rest. Sleep followed soon after, and though he called out once or twice for his late wife, missing her more each day, he otherwise slept well that night.

* * *

The day passed uneventfully, the ringing of the previous night forgotten. He decided it had all been a crazy dream, his subconscious running wild on the anniversary of his wife's death no doubt.

He spent a few minutes with Susan on the front porch, the two chatting about the weather and other mildly interesting things. She was a good woman, a caring woman, and would always ask him how he was. She knew he was hurting at the loss of his wife, even after a full year, and she always had her hand out to help him if he needed it. She was most helpful when she would give him a ride down the street to the VFW or the grocery store. He had stopped driving a few years ago, his eyes not up to the task anymore.

She was a good woman, and Walter had already decided, as he had no other heirs, to leave his house, money, and everything else he had to Susan. Besides, better her than the damn state, who would auction his possessions out piecemeal, with no regard to the late owner's attachments to the items. At least this way, he knew his beloved home would be in good hands, hopefully for many years to come.

He spent the day walking and chatting with a few neighbors, and before he realized it, the day was over and it was time for bed.

When he walked into his bedroom, gazing forlornly at the bed, something deep inside him wished his beloved Evelyn was there, waiting for him.

But, alas, the bed was empty, as it had been for a year now.

It didn't take him long to change for bed, and soon he was climbing into bed, his back flaring with twinges of pain. He pulled the covers up to his neck and tried to get comfortable. When he found his desired position, he reached out his hand to where Evelyn once laid beside him. Times like this were when he wondered if it was time for him to die too. His soul mate was gone and he was an old man with only idle days filled with nonsense to pass the time until his own day of judgment finally arrived.

He caressed the sheet, thinking back to better times, and as he reminisced, his hands resting by his side, he drifted off into a restless sleep.

* * *

*R*ing, *ring, ring!*

The inside of his head echoed like a church bell, the infernal ringing returning yet again.

Doing the same as the previous night, he reached out to the telephone on the nightstand and picked it up, placing the cold plastic receiver to his ear.

"Hello? Who the hell is this?" he demanded. Once more his eyes went to the small clock on the nightstand; it was almost four a.m. But there was no voice on the other end of the line, only a dial tone.

Then the ringing began anew, filling his head with its echo.

Dropping the phone onto the floor, he sat up in bed. He placed both hands to his ears, and as he did so, the ringing became muted, but still continued its chiming rhythm. He could feel the vibration within his mind, as if a bell was bolted to the inside of his skull.

Throwing the blankets off the bed, he charged out of the bedroom, ignoring his arthritis and bad back. Stumbling into the bathroom, he turned on the light, becoming momentarily blinded by the glare.

Drawn and tired eyes filled with sleep and terror gazed back at him from the bathroom mirror, and for a second he stared back, lost in the emptiness of his forlorn eyes. But then the ringing snapped him out of it, and he yanked open the medicine cabinet, the shelving hiding behind it now exposed. His wrinkled, frail hands reached out, brushing aside the floss, aspirin and cold medicine sitting within.

On the third shelf, in a small box, was what he needed.

Sleeping pills.

He sat on the toilet and tried to get the small foil packaging of individually packed pills open but failed miserably. He howled up at the ceiling in his frustration, eventually having to rip at the packaging with his teeth, like he was an animal fending in the garbage for sustenance. He destroyed three pills before he succeeded in opening four more. Though the side of the box recommended taking only two at a time, he ignored the warning and washed four down with a glass of water taken from the sink.

With the ringing still inside his head, making it hard to think, let alone study his situation, he stumbled back to bed. Falling into the mattress, he covered his face with the pillow. Though his ears were covered, the ringing continued, and began sobbing into his pillow, the material becoming wet with his tears.

Walter lay still for almost an hour, until the sleeping pills began to work and he eventually passed out, falling into a drug-induced slumber.

When he finally slipped from consciousness, drifting into sleep, he could still hear the dreaded ringing, as if his entire world was filled with nothing but chiming bells.

*   *   *

The next morning, Walter woke up feeling drowsy and tired, thanks to the sleeping pills suffusing his system. True, it had been a rough night, and despite the disruption in his sleep schedule, his body still had a bad habit of rousing him at five a.m. on the dot, sleeping pills or not.

He idly played with the thought of trying to sleep longer, but knew the futility of it, so he decided to get up and get dressed. Feeling groggy, like he was sleepwalking, his body fought off the rest of the drugs still floating in his system.

At seven he would go downtown to the Dunkin Donuts on the corner of Main Street and Dearborn Street and grab a cup of coffee.

If he arrived precisely at seven, his friend, Fred Prescott, would be there.

Fred was a general practitioner in the field of family medicine, and though he should have retired years ago, the man still carried on a steady practice, though he had cut down in the last two years.

Fred would always get a cup of coffee in the morning and relax with the newspaper, not needing to be in the office until nine. Though Walter could make an appointment, he knew if he was at the donut shop at seven, he could talk to Fred...and he had something serious to talk to the man about.

At five minutes to seven, Walter entered the donut shop, and of course, Fred was in his corner booth, a small coffee and a muffin sitting unobtrusively on the table in front of him. His head was buried in a newspaper, the man oblivious to the other customers moving in and out of the shop around him.

Walter stepped over to him and slid into the same booth, but on the opposite side so that he was now sitting across from the good doctor.

Fred lowered his newspaper and looked over the top of it at Walter's haggard face. "Walter, how good to see you. I didn't expect you here this morning." Fred then took a better look at Walter and frowned. "My word, you look awful. You feeling all right? You got the bug? I hear it's going around."

Walter shook his head back and forth, the gesture causing him pain in his neck. "No, I don't have the bug. I just haven't been sleeping well these past few nights."

Fred put the paper down, now fully engaged. "I see. Do you want to come in for a checkup today? Maybe we can see what's wrong with you. Check under the hood, so to speak."

Walter looked down at his hands, once again still surprised at how wrinkled and frail they looked. It seemed like it was just yesterday that his hands were like iron, strong and sure.

"I'd rather talk to you here, if it's all right," Walter said.

Fred shook his head. "No, I'm so sorry, Walter, but I can't." He checked his watch. "Actually, I have to be going in a minute or so. I have a patient coming in at eight today."

Walter's eyebrows went up. "Oh, really, since when do you see someone before nine?"

Fred chuckled. "I do when it's my wife. She needs me to go over some travel packages for our trip to Italy next month for our fortieth anniversary. She's getting them this morning from the travel agency and she's so excited that she can't wait for me to get home, so I told her to meet me at the office."

Walter only nodded. "I see. Well, congratulations on your trip."

Fred smiled in reply. "Look, if you still want me to check you out, why don't you come in around one o' clock today? I'll fit you in during my lunch hour. Shouldn't take longer than fifteen or twenty minutes."

Walter sighed, realizing Fred was offering him a favor. He nodded and said, "Okay, fine, at one. I'll be there."

Fred stood up and slid the newspaper on the table toward Walter. "Good, I'll see you at one. Here, take this and read it, will you? Relax a little bit, you look like you need to. And we'll see what's wrong with you later. All right?"

Walter only nodded. Fred patted his shoulder, and with a wave, was out the door of the donut shop and walking to his car.

Walter watched Fred leave, gazing through the glass wall of the donut shop to the street. He sat for a full two minutes, watching people walk by on their way to work before he stood up. He had better things to do today than sit in a donut shop sipping coffee and reading the paper. He had a little less than six hours before he would meet with Fred for his appointment, so he decided to try to put the previous night out of his head and focus on the here and now.

He had a few things he could do around the house to pass the time, and there was always a walk around the block. If there was still time after all of that, he might even try to sneak in a nap.

Stepping out of the donut shop, the bright sun filling the morning sky with hope and beauty, he began the trek back to his house.

* * *

Walter sat in the exam room, wearing nothing but a paper gown, while he waited anxiously for Dr. Fred Prescott to return. His legs were cold, as was his ass. They needed to turn up the heat in the room.

It was well past four and Fred had sent him to the nearby hospital where the staff had poked and prodded him until he felt like a test patient in some bizarre lab experiment. So much for fifteen to twenty minutes and he was done.

Now he was waiting for the test results, which the doctor had rushed, thanks to his connections with some of the staff on duty today at the hospital.

Walter sat quietly, swinging his wrinkled legs as they hung off the table. The wax paper lining the table was sticking to his butt cheeks, and despite the wool socks on his feet, they were growing cold too; another present from the old age fairy.

When he told Fred about the ringing in his ears, the man had frowned in curiosity. Fred had done a fair share of poking and prodding Walter himself, trying to find the reason for the odd occurrence, before sending him off to the hospital for tests.

Walter thought back to the only standout part of the exam. It was after Fred had checked his ears, blood pressure and the like. As they talked quietly, Walter trying to fill him in on everything he could think of, Fred had slid on a white latex glove.

Walter stared at the glove for a heartbeat before he pointed to it and asked, "And just what do you think you're going to do with that?"

Fred looked perplexed. "Why, I'm going to check your prostate."

Walter shook his head back and forth vehemently. "Oh no, you're not." He slapped his forehead with his left hand, signifying his head. "I told you the ringing is in my head, not my ass. Besides, I was just in here two months ago and you checked my prostate then. Thank you, but having you stick your finger in my ass once a year is more than enough for me."

Fred frowned slightly, but when he saw the look of determination on Walter's face, he gave in. "All right, fine. You're probably right. I'm just trying to be thorough."

"Well, good, let's just say we did that test and leave it at that."

Fred agreed and handed him the forms for blood work at the hospital, then he sent Walter on his way.

Now Walter was back in Fred's exam room, and for the life of him, he didn't understand why he had to take his clothes off again and put on another ridiculous paper gown.

The door opened and Fred Prescott walked in. He saw Walter in the gown and gestured to the clothes on the chair beside him. "Oh, sorry about that, Walter. My nurse didn't realize why you were here, and that you were here once already today. You can get dressed if you want."

Walter slid off the table, his ass cheeks pulling the wax paper along with him. In frustration, he pulled it away from him, wrinkled it up, and tossed it into the corner angrily.

Fred watched it all impassively at first and then Walter realized the man was staring, so he calmed down.

"Sorry, Fred, it's just that I've been waiting here for what seems like forever and you don't know the things going through my mind." He picked up his clothes and placed them on the exam table.

Sitting down in the only chair in the room, Fred nodded. "It's quite all right, Walter, really. I have your test results right here."

Walter began dressing while Fred worked his way through the sheaf of paper, reading the results to himself.

"Well, and?" Walter asked as he slid his right leg into his pants, his knee joint protesting the action.

"Well, at first I thought it might be tinnitus, but there doesn't seem to be any sign of a middle-ear infection. You said you're not suffering from symptoms such as a fever, an earache or an unusual amount of pressure in your ears, correct?"

Walter nodded.

"And you said you don't hear the ringing all the time?"

Walter nodded again, now a look of concern crossing his face. He didn't like where the questions were going.

"Hmm, then it's not tinnitus. If it was, the ringing would be constant, and you just said that isn't the case."

"That's right. It only seems to happen at night when I'm asleep. It keeps waking me up and it only happens around three or four in the morning."

"Well, according to these results everything else is fine. There are no fractures or signs of a concussion. There doesn't seem to be anything wrong with your spine. No tumors or any other foreign bodies."

"Other foreign bodies? Like what?" Walter asked.

"Hmm, let me see," Fred said, thinking on it while tapping his lips with a pen. "I'll give you an example. There was this fella last year that came in to see me. He had a bullet lodged in his skull. Evidently, some idiot shot his gun into the air like those rednecks do when they're celebrating something. Well, what goes up must come down, and this poor guy was sleeping in his hammock in his yard when the .22 caliber bullet entered the top of his head just a little above the ear. At the time, the guy thought he had gotten hit with a stick or a rock or something. There was a miniscule amount of blood and just a small entry wound no larger than the tip of a pencil. Well, after that he started to get headaches, and when they did an MRI, do you know what they found?"

"The bullet," Walter replied flatly.

Fred nodded. "Yup. Went in just enough to give the guy headaches, but that's all. "They operated and took it out and the guy's fine to this day."

"Huh, imagine that. Okay, what else could it be if it's not a bullet or a foreign object?"

"Well, let's see. Your cholesterol is a little high and I don't like the look of your sodium count, not to mention your heart sounds a little rough; it's possible you may have a heart murmur. We'll have to do some more tests on that, but you are in your eighties, after all. Other than that, you appear to be in fairly good health."

"Then what the hell am I supposed to do? Am I going crazy?"

Fred moved closer to his friend and patted him on the shoulder. "No, of course not. I'm sure there's a rational enough reason for this to be happening. We just need to find out what it is."

Fred began thinking, chewing his lip idly, and then his eyes lit up with an idea.

"Listen, don't tell anybody I told you to do this, but why don't you try going to a chiropractor? I knew someone who thought they were suffering from tinnitus, and after they had their neck adjusted, the ringing went away."

Walter pondered the suggestion and then shrugged. "Okay, fine, if I don't get a good night's sleep tonight, that's what I'll do tomorrow." He moved a little closer to Fred. "So, do you have anyone you can recommend?"

Fred frowned, but stood up and walked to the door. "I'll have to check my referral book. I'll be right back."

Walter waved him away and finished dressing.

Maybe he would be fine tonight. Maybe there would be no ringing. He would just have to wait and see.

* * *

It was exactly three-thirty in the morning when Walter was pulled from his slumber.

The ringing was back, filling his head like a parade of bells.

He lay in the lonely bed, staring up at the darkened ceiling. His hands were at his sides, both balled into fists of rage. Though the arthritis in his knuckles screamed at him, he ignored it, the rage he felt more than enough to override the pain.

On a whim, he sat up, reached over, and picked up the telephone receiver.

"Hello, is anyone there?"

But of course there was nothing but a dial tone.

"Goddamn it," he screamed into his pillow. "Tomorrow, bright and early, I'm going to the chiropractor!"

He lay back down and stared at the ceiling in frustrated agony as the ringing of a mystical telephone continued in his head all through the rest of the night.

*   *   *

He arrived at the chiropractor at two-thirty in the afternoon, after calling that morning for an appointment.

Dr. Valmont had been able to squeeze him in after someone had called in a cancellation at the last minute. The doctor had especially wanted to help him after Walter had shared his difficulty with him.

It also didn't hurt that Walter's insurance would cover the entire visit with no questions asked.

Walter sat in the waiting room, counting the minutes until he would be called in to see the doctor. As he waited, his eyes kept wandering to the secretary seated at her desk, typing away. She was a pretty thing in her twenties, with flowing blonde hair and a bosom that would stop traffic. Every now and then she would look up and see him watching her. She would smile at him and then go back to her typing.

He chuckled softly at that. Though in his eighties, Walter still couldn't help but admire the young ladies. He found it odd that no matter how old he became, he was still attracted to the same women and age group as when he was in his twenties.

Though sex was a thing of the past, he still couldn't help but admire the curves of a woman or the way her buttocks swayed when she walked. Not that he would have ever contemplated cheating on his late wife. No, he had loved her far too much. But what was wrong with admiring other women for their beauty?

Even if the pretty secretary had somehow been attracted to him, and not thought of him as a dirty old man for admiring her in a sexual way, he would have posed her no harm.

The only way he was going to get his penis hard was with a bottle of Viagra, and if he did that, he would probably end up killing himself from a heart attack.

No, his sexual days were most definitely over, but still, the way she moved in her small dress couldn't help but make his stomach flutter like he was a teenager.

Finally, the doctor called him, opening the door that led deeper into the building, smiling at his secretary as he waited for Walter to cross the room.

From the smile Dr. Valmont flashed his secretary, Walter couldn't help but wonder if the doctor was banging her on the side. That would surely explain why he had such a pretty young thing for a secretary. But then again, maybe she was just an excellent receptionist.

Walter and the doctor chatted lightly while they walked down the small hallway with doors lining each side. When Walter was escorted into one of the rooms, he was told to take off his shirt and lie face down on the table centered in the middle of the room. There was a padded opening for his face so he wouldn't suffocate as the doctor worked on him.

When he was good and comfortable, Dr. Valmont began working, poking, prodding and rubbing.

"So you say you have a ringing in your ears?" the doctor asked as he pulled back on Walter's arm.

Wincing slightly in pain, Walter nodded an affirmative, and then realizing the futility of the gesture, he grunted a yes.

"I see, well it does seem that your spine is a little off alignment. Let me see if I can realign it for you, hmm?"

Dr. Valmont placed one hand on Walter's neck, another on his shoulder, and began pushing.

Walter grunted on the table and finally could stand the discomfort no more. "Enough, Doctor, I'm, not a goddamn chicken wing. What the hell are you trying to do, make a wish?"

Dr. Valmont backed off and Walter rolled off the table to standing up, bare-chested in the cold room.

"I'm very sorry, Mr. Whitaker, but I'm only doing what I have to if you want me to realign your spine."

Walter leaned over, picked up his shirt, and began dressing. "Look, I think this was a bad idea. Forget it. My damn spine is fine."

"But, Mr. Whitaker, I'm sure I can help you," Dr. Valmont pleaded.

"Bah, whatever is happening to me, it's in my head, not my spine. I'll thank you to leave me be." Finished dressing, and with his coat and cane in hand, he opened the door to leave.

"Look, thanks for trying, Doctor, but I'm an old man. I'm truly afraid you'll snap me like a dry piece of toast. Thank you anyway." With a curt smile, he began walking to the exit.

Dr. Valmont followed. "I'm truly sorry I couldn't be of more help, Mr. Whitaker, but I have to tell you there will still be a bill for today's session."

Walter waved to the man. "Fine, just send me the difference from whatever the insurance doesn't pay for. Good day." He smiled briefly to the secretary as he exited the office.

Oh well, at least he'd tried, he thought. Besides, maybe the poking and prodding the doctor had assaulted him with had already done the job and finally silenced the infernal ringing.

He guessed he would just have to wait for tonight to find out.

* * *

When Walter went to bed that night, he found he couldn't sleep. He didn't want to, he was far too restless. For the past few days, every time he closed his eyes, he found himself being thrown awake again by the constant ringing.

As he lay alone in his bed, he wondered if the ringing would come tonight. Though he prayed it didn't, there was another part of him that almost hoped it did. In the past year, his life had been without meaning. Since the loss of his wife, Evelyn, everything had seemed so washed out to him.

Food had become tasteless and the sky seemed a little more faded than it used to look. The truth of it was that he wondered if he really wanted to continue going on anymore. His best friend had died and now he was so alone.

But he would never kill himself. Oh no, that would be ridiculous, he would just have to wait for nature to take its course and finish him off the old fashioned way.

The only thing was, with his luck, he would end up living until he was ninety.

A truck rumbled by outside on the street and he was pulled from his reverie. The ceiling hovered over him, and he gazed up at it for the hundred-thousandth time since he had moved into the house all those years ago.

He knew every crack and crevice, every nuance of the ceiling. He had repainted it many years ago and now, as he studied the paint job intently, he saw every brushstroke and curve he had done in the past. The light fixture in the middle of the ceiling had some paint on the brass base bolted to the ceiling. Evidently, he hadn't done as good a job of taping up the fixture as he thought.

He almost wanted to stand up on the bed and try to scratch the paint off the fixture with his fingernail, but knew he would probably lose his balance and kill himself in the process.

So he stared at the paint on the light, a memory of his sloppiness from all those years ago. The minutes ticked by, soon turning into hours, and before he knew it, the clock was changing to three a.m.

He stared at it, lying on his side, waiting for the inevitable to happen. When the clock had reached three fifty a.m., he was actually beginning to hope his ordeal was over. Perhaps whatever was happening to him had finally stopped for good. But when the clock changed to three fifty-one a.m., the first ring sounded in his head.

"*Noooo!*" he screamed at the top of his lungs, throwing his pillow at the clock, as if the inanimate object could somehow accept the blame for what was happening to him.

The pillow struck the top of the nightstand, the clock and phone falling to the floor in a clatter. The small lamp teetered on the edge for a moment, as if it was deciding if it should join its friends, and then it fell off the night stand to land on top of the clock and phone.

Walter sat up in bed, the ringing continuing in his mind, and he squeezed his hands on each side of his ears to try and stop it. Of course this did nothing but muffle the noise. On the floor, the phone, now off the hook, began beeping.

At first he thought it was in his head, but soon realized this noise was external. Reaching down with a twinge of pain in his back, he picked up the phone and placed the receiver back on its base, but left the receiver and cradle on the floor.

There, at least one annoying noise had been silenced.

With a weary sigh, he picked up the lamp and pillow, but the clock he left on the floor with the phone. With a frustrated sigh, he laid down. With his eyes once again staring at the ceiling, a few tears of helplessness rolling down his cheeks, he lay quietly while the ringing continued in his head.

The right corner of his lip twitched slightly, and deep in his mind, something cracked. He knew, at that precise moment, that if he couldn't stop the ringing soon, he would end up doing something drastic.

But there would be a bright side to this action. At least he would get to Heaven quicker and join his beloved Evelyn.

* * *

The next morning, Walter stumbled into the Dunkin Donuts, hoping to find Dr. Fred Prescott at his usual table as the man enjoyed his morning coffee.

He was in luck and Fred was where he always was, a creature of habit if there ever was one. Walter moved up to the table and plopped down without an invitation.

Fred lowered his newspaper and his jaw dropped slightly when he saw how his old friend looked. "My God, Walter, you look terrible," he said in mild shock.

It was true, Walter had looked better. His eyes were drawn and he had large bags below his eyes. His face seemed to sag more than usual and his gray hair was a mess, a tangled hive of string on his head—what was left of it, anyway.

But it was the eyes that were the worst. The eyes which were usually bright and friendly were now glossy and unfocused.

"No, shit, Fred. Is that an expert opinion? Am I going to get a bill for that diagnosis?"

Fred took his friend's gruffness and lack of health into consideration and ignored the jibe. He assumed what the reason for Walter's appearance was, but wanted to confirm it, so he leaned over the table to speak quietly. "Is it that ringing in your head? Is it still happening?"

Walter slapped his right hand on the table, causing Fred's coffee cup to jump a half inch, but not spilling. With all the sleep he had lost in the past few days, he was becoming irritable and grouchy. The classic stereotype of the crotchety old man.

"Of course it's that damn ringing. I tell you, Fred, if it doesn't stop, I'm going to have to do something crazy. I can't take it anymore. It's driving me mad!" His voice went up in pitch, causing some of the other patrons in the donut shop to glance at him curiously. Fred merely nodded at them with a polite smile and the patrons decided it was nothing.

Fred reached out a hand and placed it on Walter's right wrist. "Look, old friend, there has to be something we can do about this." His forehead creased as he thought about the situation. "Okay, tell you what. We've been looking at this like it's a medical problem, right?"

Walter only grunted.

"Okay then, what about if we look at it like it's psychological. Maybe it has to do with stress or something in that category."

"I'm not crazy, Fred, and I'm not going to see a damn head-shrinker, if that's what you're suggesting."

Fred waved his hand in the air, dismissing the idea before it could take root in Walter's mind. "No, of course not, that's not what I meant. Now, please, tell me exactly how the ringing sounds. Is it like a church bell or maybe a car horn?"

Walter shook his head. "No, damn it. I told you before that it's exactly like a telephone. Exactly."

Fred creased his lips as he concentrated on the idea of the ringing. "A telephone you say? Okay, then I have only one piece of advice to give you," he said and leaned back in the booth, his face looking like a man who had solved a great mystery.

Walter stared at Fred, his face contorted with aggravation. "Yes, well, out with it then. What's your advice?"

Fred said each word carefully, almost as if he didn't believe his own advice. "Well, if it truly is a telephone ringing in you head, perhaps it's your subconscious or something trying to contact you in some bizarre way. If there truly is something trying to get in touch with you, then did you ever think to just answer it?"

*   *   *

For the rest of the day, Walter walked around in a daze. He couldn't stop thinking about Fred's suggestion.

Just answer it.

If it was the ringing of a telephone inside his mind, then could he just answer it and find out if there was actually anything on the other end of the mystical line?

But what if there wasn't? What if there was no caller in his head and the ringing just went on and on until he finally went insane. Questions such as these filled his mind the entire day, but eventually the day ended and night fell across the land.

A little past eight p.m., he proceeded to get ready for bed. Though anxious about what might come later that night, he also felt a sense of calm as if he was finally in control of the situation.

Crawling into bed, he reached over to Evelyn's side of the bed, wishing for the millionth time that she was still with him. As he laid his head down on his pillow, he let out a long, weary sigh.

He was so tired.

He closed his eyes.

Sleep wouldn't come at first. It was like a stray piece of paper blowing in the midst of a heavy wind, always out of reach, yet always in sight. But as he slowed his breathing and relaxed a little more each hour, eventually he fell into a restless slumber.

Dreams of his wife filled his mind; times when they had been young and so very happy.

Just as the dreams were getting good, a ringing fractured the tableaux of happiness and he found himself falling back to reality. Opening his eyes in the darkness, he saw nothing unusual, but the ringing had most definitely returned.

It was like an old friend visiting after months away, Walter thought. He smiled.

Thinking back to what Fred Prescott had said, he decided to give it a try. He visualized a phone sitting on a table. The phone was ringing, the same chiming filling his mind now. He pictured himself walking over to the phone, and ever so carefully, picking up the receiver. When he did this, the ringing stopped, and silence descended once more.

In the real world, his body lay stretched out on the bed, perfectly still, his chest rising and falling in cadence to his steady breathing. Deep inside his mind, he placed the receiver to his ear, and with a dry mouth, he swallowed slightly, cleared his throat, and asked, "Uhm, hello? Is anyone there?"

There were a few clicks and beeps on the other end that lasted two heartbeats, but then a woman's voice came on the line. Her voice was nasally, reminding him of operators from the 1950s

"Ah yes, finally. Is this Mr. Walter Whitaker?" the voice asked in a formal voice. There was no inflection in the voice, only a business attitude. Walter swallowed again, his throat moving with the motion, and he nodded his head. Then, realizing he was talking on a phone, he said, "Uh, yes. Yes, this is Walter Whitaker. Can I ask who you are?"

"That is unimportant, Mr. Whitaker. All you need to know is we have been trying to get in touch with you for almost a week. You've been causing quite a problem in scheduling in your refusal to answer the line."

Not knowing how to react, Walter fell back on his manners. "I'm sorry? I didn't know what the ringing was."

"That's irrelevant, Mr. Whitaker; at least you've finally answered. Now, I have a person to person call for you. Do you accept the call?"

Though not quite understanding why, Walter knew he wanted to accept the phone call. In fact, he knew he had wanted to receive this call for almost a year, but had no way of understanding when it would come or how it would finally show itself.

In his mind, he nodded and said, "Yes, operator, yes, I'll accept the call."

"Excellent, Mr. Whitaker, excellent, and before I transfer you, I have a message for you. Your wife told me to tell you that she's waiting for you and she'll see you soon and that she loves you very much."

With his real body still lying on the bed, tears of sadness mixed with joy seeped out of his closed eyes, and deep inside his mind, Walter smiled. "Thank you for that operator, thank you."

"You're welcome, Mr. Whitaker. Now please hold, I'm transferring the call now."

Walter stood by the phone in his mind, patiently waiting for the call to be transferred.

Three heartbeats later, and there was another click, followed by the sound of someone breathing softly. "Hello, Walter, it's good to finally talk to you," a deep voice said, the voice filled with sympathy and love. "I've been trying to contact you for quite a while now. It's time to come home."

Walter grinned happily in his mind. "I know that now, I'm sorry, I didn't understand. I've wanted to talk with you, too." His smile grew wider. "I'm ready. In fact, I've been ready for a while."

Lying on the bed, Walter's lips creased into a slight smile and his breathing began to slow, his chest rising and falling with less speed.

In the darkness, his chest rose one final time, then was still. But on his lips, there was the mere hint of a smile, as if upon passing, he had been thinking of something wonderful.

The ringing would not return. It had been finally silenced, for the call had been answered.

Now and forever.

CLAN OF THE BIGFOOT

BY ANTHONY GIANGREGORIO
LIVING DEAD PRESS.COM

SUNSET
OF THE DEAD

ANTHONY GIANGREGORIO

CREATURE FEATURE
A MONSTER ANTHOLOGY

EDITED BY
ANTHONY GIANGREGORIO

www.ingramcontent.com/pod-product-compliance
Lightning Source LLC
Chambersburg PA
CBHW071000120726
47910CB00004B/1316